SUDDEN DEATH

Blade brought the SEAL to a stop, turning the transport, angling it across the road, Hickok's side to the fleeing motorcycle.

Hickok hastily rolled down his window and raised his Henry, sighting carefully.

"You can't," Joshua claimed.

"He tried to kill us," Blade reminded Joshua.

"Not in the back!" Joshua protested.

"We have no choice!" Blade declared, watching the other driver speed off. If Hickok didn't fire soon, even he wouldn't be able to make the shot.

"No!" Joshua shouted, flinging himself forward, lunging for Hickok.

Geronimo reacted instantly, clutching Joshua, restraining him.

"No!" Joshua struggled to break free. "He's another human being!"

"Not any more," Hickok said softly. He inhaled, held the breath, and squeezed the trigger.

Also by David Robbins:

BLOOD CULT
THE WERELING
THE ENDWORLD SERIES #1: THE FOX RUN
THE ENDWORLD SERIES #3: THE TWIN
    CITIES RUN
THE ENDWORLD SERIES #4: THE
    KALISPELL RUN

DAVID ROBBINS

ENDWORLD

THIEF RIVER FALLS RUN

LEISURE BOOKS ∞ NEW YORK CITY

To Joshua,
for all the happiness

A LEISURE BOOK

Published by

Dorchester Publishing Co., Inc.
6 East 39th Street
New York, NY 10016

Printed in the United States of America

THIEF RIVER
FALLS RUN

1

The buckskin-clad gunman crouched and spun, his hands dropping to his pearl-handled revolvers, one in a leather holster on each hip, his long blond locks waving in the wind, his keen blue eyes scanning the field below him, searching for the source of the noise he had just heard.

Someone had coughed.

A full moon illuminated the field, kept cleared of all brush, trees, and other vegetation to prevent any foes, human or otherwise, from covertly assaulting the thirty-acre plot called the Home by those who lived within the encircling brick walls. The Family, as they designated themselves, took extraordinary precautions to insure its safety: the twenty-foot-high walls were topped with barbed wire and a rampart for patrolling purposes, a wide moat was channeled around the base of the wall, within the compound; and the entire Home was continually guarded by an elite corps of skilled, thoroughly trained fighters known as Warriors.

"Hickok, did you hear that?" whispered a small, wiry man as he scurried along the rampart in the gunman's direction.

"Sure did, pard," acknowledged Hickok, nodding.

The second man stopped at Hickok's side. "Came from the edge of the field," he stated. His brown eyes studied the forest, dimly visible as a looming dark mass, one hundred and fifty yards distant. "Near the trees. We were fortunate the wind carried the sound this far. Any orders?"

Hickok mentally pondered the situation. Should they investigate the cough now, or leave it until daylight? What would Blade do at a time like this?

The Warriors were divided into four sections, or Triads, comprised of three members each. Designated the Alpha, Beta, Gamma, and Omega Triads, they were entrusted with the defense of the Home and the protection of the Family. While each Triad had an appointed head, all of the Warriors were under the leadership of the Alpha Triad, and each of the twelve Warriors was specifically responsible to Blade, the chief of Alpha Triad and the commander of all Family Warriors.

Blast! Hickok thoughtfully stroked his blond moustache, debating on a course of action. Blade was recuperating from an infection his body had developed, a reaction to the dozens of cuts and slashes inflicted by a deadly wolverine during their battle with the Trolls. He was probably asleep at this late hour, dreaming of his beloved Jenny. Lucky him!

"Should we alert Geronimo?" the other man asked, running his right hand through his black hair, relieved as the breeze picked up, cooling his sweaty brow. The July night was warm and muggy.

"Nope," Hickok laconically responded. "Would take too long, Rikki. Geronimo is way over on the east wall."

The Alpha Triad consisted of Blade, Geronimo, and Hickok. With Blade recovering from the infection, another Warrior had volunteered to take his place on guard duty. Rikki-Tikki-Tavi, the Beta Triad leader, clutched a long black scabbard in his left hand. He pointed it at the distant woods. "I'll go myself, if you like."

"I'm going," Hickok announced, making his decision. "Alone."

"I should go along." Rikki-Tikki-Tavi offered.

"I'm going alone," Hickok repeated, carefully moving along the rampart until he was in the center of the western wall, directly above a closed drawbridge.

Rikki followed on his heels. "Could be a trap," he said, voicing his concern. "Could be some more scavengers," he noted, referring to an attack by a roving band of marauders several years before, an assault the Family successfully repelled.

"Could be," Hickok agreed, glancing down. Imbedded in the concrete at his moccasined feet was a thick steel ring. Attached to the ring, coiled in a large pile on the rampart, was a stout rope.

"You'll need a backup," Rikki contended.

"No, thanks," Hickok declined. He lifted the rope. At this one point, the barbed wire was deliberately spaced to permit one person to pass over the edge of the rampart.

"You don't know who or what is out there," Rikki stated, his tone reflecting his annoyance.

"Doesn't matter," Hickok informed him.

"It's against standard Warrior procedure," Rikki added.

Hickok shrugged, peered over the top of the wall, and tossed the rope down the wall.

"You're taking a needless risk." Rikki wouldn't let the matter drop. "You could be killed."

Hickok paused in the act of climbing over the side. He stared into Rikki's dark eyes. "I don't care, pard. I just don't care." He pushed off.

Rikki-Tikki-Tavi knelt and watched his friend slowly lower himself to the ground in front of the drawbridge. So! What Blade and Geronimo had said about Hickok was true. With the death of the woman he loved, at the hands of the Trolls, Hickok was displaying signs of outright recklessness with regard to his personal safety. The Family's supreme gunman seemed normal otherwise, but Blade believed Hickok was a simmering volcano waiting for the right catalyst to trigger an eruption. Rikki vividly recalled the tormented expression on Hickok's face when they had buried the woman. Joan, her name had been, and rumor had it she was Hickok's first true love.

Hickok reached the bare earth below the drawbridge and waved once to Rikki before jogging across the field in the direction of the cough. He knew he should present as small a target as possible to potential ambushers, but his suppressed grief negated his extensive Warrior training and he ran upright, exposed, almost hoping he would see the flash of a firearm and feel the impact of a slug ripping through his body.

The wind increased, the natural elements working in his favor. The breeze was blowing the sounds he made toward the Home, and away from whoever was lurking in the forest at the end of the field.

A sudden thought brought Hickok up short. What if it were Trolls? Many had escaped, and they'd want revenge on the Family. Involuntarily, he gripped his revolvers, his cherished Colt Pythons.

Someone coughed again.

May the Spirit smile on me, Hickok prayed. He lowered his body, running in a half-crouch, moving cautiously now, a grim smile on his face. Whoever was out there was due west, a bit to his right. Please let it be Trolls! He owed them. He owed them real bad.

Hickok slowed as he neared the trees, listening, his senses primed. The leaves were rustling in the wind, some of the branches creaking and rubbing against one another. Good. Perfect cover. He tensed, expecting a shot, and darted into the woods, stopping behind the first large tree he reached. Surely they had seen him coming. He leaned against the trunk, waiting.

Nothing.

What was going on here?

The coughing abruptly started up, a veritable spasm, a series of wheezing gasps and choking groans.

Sounds like the dude is sick, Hickok reasoned. He estimated the distance at fifteen to twenty yards. The brush was thick, providing ample concealment. He lowered his body to the earth and began crawling.

A twig snapped behind him.

Hickok froze. Blast his stupidity! He should have expected there would be more than one. Had they seen him?

"Did you get a fix on that?" a gruff voice whispered.

Hickok twisted, craning his neck, confident he was hidden in the tall grass.

There were three of them. Big men. Armed with rifles. Two to his left, one to his right, the nearest ten yards away.

"I know I heard it," a second man replied in a hushed voice.

Were they talking about him? Hickok wondered.

The coughing started up again.

"There!" the first man exclaimed. All three wore green uniforms.

The three men stalked their prey, passing Hickok, intent on their target.

What the blazes was going on here? They were after the cougher. Why? Who were they? Even in the subdued light, Hickok could see they were well dressed, their clothes appearing new and somehow different from the homemade attire the Family wore. Each man held a polished rifle and wore an automatic pistol strapped to his waist. Who are these guys? Hickok asked himself.

Only one thing to do.

Hickok waited until they were a safe distance ahead, then pursued them, crawling through the grass and skirting any bushes or trees in his path. They were proceeding very deliberately, actually inching forward now, and he easily kept them in sight.

The poor slob with the nasty cough wheezed once more.

Hickok saw the three men quickly rush ahead, beyond his vision. He heard the commotion of a brief struggle, then a solid blow landing.

"Got you!" someone declared enthusiastically.

Hickok rose, keeping stooped over, and hastened forward until he reached a tree about six yards from a small clearing. The men were standing over another person, prone on the ground, grinning and smiling.

"You really gave us a run for our money," the gruff voice said. "I've got to hand it to you."

"Answer him," snapped the tallest of the men, kicking the body in the side, eliciting a moan from the unfortunate victim.

"Yeah, bitch!" teased the third man. "We can't hear you!"

Bitch? Hickok edged around the tree.

"Stand up, woman!" the gruff voice ordered. "I have some questions for you!"

Hickok's view of the woman was blocked by the legs of the men. He heard her sob and mumble something.

"Can't hear you, squaw," the gruff voice stated, "and I need to know where the little one is."

Little one? Squaw?

"If you don't start talking," the tallest uniform snarled, "I'm going to break your bones one by one." He brutally kicked the woman one more time.

Enough was enough.

Hickok took two steps forward, his thumbs casually hooked in his gunbelt.

"Stand up, damn you!" the gruff voice commanded.

"Excuse me, gentlemen. . ." Hickok said quietly.

The three men whirled, startled, momentarily off guard.

" . . . I reckon it's useless to point out how atrocious your manners are." Hickok grinned at them.

The uniforms overcame their initial shock, bringing their rifles into play.

"Waste him!" the gruff voice bellowed.

Hickok drew, his hands a blur, the Pythons out and leveled faster than the eye could blink, held low, near his waist, the .357's booming and bucking, his aim unerring.

The gruff voice clutched at his face as a bullet penetrated his forehead and exploded through the back of his head.

The third uniform was caught in the right eye. He screamed while he fell, his rifle clattering beside him.

As the Family's firearms expert and deadliest gunfighter, Hickok taught firearms use and safety to novice Warriors and the small children. Everyone in the Family was required to become familiar with guns; their lives could depend on the knowledge. Most of them did not utilize firearms in their daily activities, so they were asked to take annual refresher courses. In a world where survival of the fittest was the cardinal rule, the Family needed to be prepared for any eventuality, including a mass assault on its Home. At the classes he conducted, Hickok stressed his fundamental law of marksmanship. "Go for the head," he invariably told them. "Anywhere else and they can still come at you. Get their brain and you put them completely out of commission." He did allow several exceptions. "If you don't have time to aim for the head and you're not a great shot," he had instructed one class, "if the head shot is obstructed in some way, or it's personal, then shoot anywhere you think will be effective." In all his years as a Warrior, Hickok could count on the fingers of one hand the number of times he had not gone for the head. Most of them were for personal reasons.

Like now.

The tallest uniform had his rifle to his shoulder when the first shot splintered his left knee. He shrieked and dropped his gun, staggering when the second bullet burst his right kneecap, blood and bone spraying his leg. His eyes focused on the blond gunman as he stumbled to the ground, silently pleading to be spared.

"You shouldn't have kicked her, pard," Hickok stated sternly. "I noticed you enjoy inflicting pain. How do you feel now, when the shoe is on the other foot?"

"Please . . ." the man begged.

"Sorry, pard," Hickok said harshly, "but I can't abide people who like hurting others. There's enough anguish in this warped world as it is."

"Please . . ." the tall uniform repeated.

Both Pythons blasted the man into eternity.

Hickok twirled his Colts and slid them into their respective holsters. "Well, what have we here?" He knelt next to the woman, studying her.

She was lying on her left side, curled up, her arms held close to her chest. Her clothes were finely crafted homemade buckskins, embroidered on the back with a colorful representation of a rainbow. Luxuriant black hair descended to the small of her back. Her eyes were closed, and she was breathing heavily, almost gasping.

"You don't sound too good, sister," Hickok commented. He placed his right hand on her forehead. The woman was burning up.

"Take your filthy hand off her!" someone shouted in a high, thin voice. The patter of feet running came from behind him.

Hickok twisted, his left Python already clear, the hammer drawn back, his finger tightening on the trigger. Only his superb self-control enabled him to turn the barrel aside at the last possible instant, the shot plowing into the ground.

The young girl kept coming. An exact copy of the older woman, about ten years of age, she furiously swung her tiny fists at the gunman as she closed in, tears streaking her contorted face.

"Leave my mommy alone!" she yelled.

Hickok felt several of her blows land as he holstered his left Colt and grabbed for her wrists.

"Why won't you leave us alone?" the girl wailed.

Hickok was able to grip both her wrists. She fought on, a veritable wildcat, tossing and kicking him in the legs.

"Whoa there, girl! Calm down! I'm not going to hurt you or your mom."

"Liar!" the girl disputed him. "You're just like the others! You want to kill us!" She managed to place a particularly effective kick on his right shin.

"Ouch! Will you cut it out? Stop for just a second."

The girl was slowing down, winded, her emotional momentum exhausted.

"That's more like it." Hickok slowly stood, retaining his hold on her wrists. His shin was throbbing. "I'm not going to hurt you," he re-affirmed.

Sniffling, the girl looked up at him. "How can I trust you?" she asked weakly.

"Didn't I just kill the men who were after your mom and you?"

She stopped crying and glanced at the dead men. "I saw you do it," she said softly.

Hickok flinched, wishing she hadn't. "So don't you think it means I'm on your side?"

"Maybe," she reluctantly admitted. "Mom says we can't trust anyone, though."

Hickok opted to change the subject and forestall another attack on his shins. "Your mom seems to be sick."

The girl stared at her mother and nodded. "She is, mister. Has been for weeks. We couldn't stop, though. She said the bad men would catch up with us."

"If I release you," Hickok said, "will you promise not to kick me again?"

"Okay."

Hickok gingerly freed her hands. "I know some people who can help your mother," he informed her.

"Where are they?" she questioned.

Hickok found himself admiring her frank and fearless attitude. "Over there." He pointed at the Home, partially visible through the trees.

"We saw it earlier," the girl mentioned. "Mom said we couldn't get too close because bad people might live there."

"Only good people live there," Hickok assured her. "My people. We're called the Family. Some of our people are Healers. They can help your mom."

"You'd do that for us?" she asked incredulously.

"Of course. A pard of mine, named Joshua, says all of us are children of the Creator. That makes us all brothers and sisters. It means we're supposed to help each other."

"I don't know . . ." she said doubtfully. "I better ask mom." She dropped to her knees and leaned over her mother. "Mom? Mom? Can you hear me? This man says he can help us? What do I do?"

The woman only groaned.

"Looks like your mom is in no shape to make a decision," Hickok observed. "It's up to you."

"I don't know . . ." The girl bit her lower lip, her brow furrowed.

"What's your name?" Hickok asked her.

"I'm Star. Who are you?"

Hickok extended his right hand, "Folks call me Hickok."

Star stared at his hand. "What's that for?"

"For shaking. It's a custom when you meet someone new."

"We do this," Star stated. She stood and raised her right hand, palm out. "Peace, Hickok," she declared solemnly.

Hickok suppressed an impulse to chuckle. He followed her example. "Peace, Star."

"I guess I'll have to trust you," Star sighed. "I've got no other choice."

Hickok knelt and placed his arms under the woman's body.

"What are you doing?" Star quickly demanded.

"Relax. I've got to carry your mom across the field to the Home. The sooner we have the Healers examine her, the better."

"Okay."

The woman was light, not much over one hundred pounds. Hickok lifted her with ease. "What's your mom's name?"

"Rainbow," Star answered.

"Do tell." He moved through the brush, the girl at his side, her worried gaze fixed on her unconscious mother.

They reached the field, the bright moon overhead.

"Who's that?" Sarah suddenly asked.

Hickok followed the direction of her gaze and spotted a figure coming toward them from the Home. He recognized the fluid, controlled movements of the Family's martial arts master. "That's a pard of mine," he said to Star. "His name is Rikki-Tikki-Tavi."

"You're kidding, right?" Star replied.

"Ask him if you don't believe me."

The Beta Triad Warrior reached them, his scabbard gripped in his right hand. "I heard the shots," he explained, "and presumed you needed assistance. Obviously not."

"Say, mister." Star looked up at Rikki. "Is your name really Rikki-Tavi-Tikki?"

"Rikki-Tikki-Tavi, at your service." Rikki bowed and swept his left arm in a grandiose flourish.

"Where'd you get a name like that?" Star wanted to know.

"Out of a book . . ." Rikki began to answer.

"Oh?" Star clapped her hands, excited. "You have books here?"

"Hundreds of thousands," Rikki responded. "The man who built our Home knew we would require knowledge to persevere in the world after World War Three. We have a magnificent library."

"I just love books," Star said delightedly. "We only have a couple of dozen and I've read all of them."

"Who taught you to read?" Rikki asked her.

"My mother," Star stated, reaching up and taking her mother's limp right hand.

"Who happens to be very ill," Hickok interjected. "We've got to get her to the Healers as quickly as possible." He led the way, walking briskly in the direction of the drawbridge.

"You were telling me about your name," Star reminded Rikki as they followed the gunman.

"I picked it from a book about an animal called a mongoose. This animal was responsible for guarding its human family from some vicious snakes. I'm a Warrior, and I've been trained to protect my Family, so I thought the name was highly appropriate. I selected it at my Naming, on my sixteenth birthday." Rikki turned his head slightly, the better to attune his hearing to the gusting wind.

"Your Naming?" Star asked.

"Kurt Carpenter, the man who constructed the Home, wanted his descendants to appreciate their historical roots. We're encouraged to scour the library books for any name we prefer. It's bestowed on us during a special ceremony on our sixteenth birthday."

"Do many pick a name as weird as yours?" Star inquired.

"Not many," Rikki admitted, grinning. "You sure ask a lot of questions. What's your name?"

"Star."

"How old are you?"

Star squared her shoulders and elevated her chin. "I'm a mature twelve, almost thirteen."

Rikki chuckled.

"That's what Rainbow, my mom, says," Star stated stiffly.

"I believe you . . . ." Rikki paused, turning. The breeze brought a peculiar shuffling sound to his ears.

"Is something wrong?" Star questioned him.

Rikki glanced at Hickok. The gunman was at least ten yards in front of them and making haste for the Home.

"What is it?" Star demanded, sensing his concern.

"Run and catch up with Hickok," Rikki told her. He faced the forest and detected a large black hump moving across the background of the rustling trees.

"Why? What's wrong?" Star stubbornly persisted.

"Do as I tell you. Now!" Rikki said harshly.

Star ran off.

Rikki-Tikki-Tavi watched the hump cross the field, directly on their trail. He would make his stand right where he was, giving Hickok and Star ample time to reach the Home and safety. What was it? he wondered. A mutate, one of the deformed, pus-covered horrors now proliferating everywhere as a result of the War? Mutates were former mammals, reptiles, or amphibians, changed into ravenous monstrosities by a mysterious, unknown process. No one, not even wise Plato, the leader of the Family, knew the cause, the agent responsible for transforming ordinary creatures into devilish demons. Were mutates the result of the radiation released during the Big Blast, as the Family referred to World War Three, or the consequence of the widespread use of chemical weaponry during the predominantly nuclear war?

The black hump was proceeding slowly. Several thin appendages were visible, periodically waving in the air.

Rikki doubted this was a mutate. Mutates craved flesh, and their appetites were insatiable. They attacked and devoured anything and everything they encountered, in a frenzy of blood lust, without hesitation. The thing wasn't coming fast enough.

As if in response to his thought, the hump increased its speed.

Rikki assumed the Kokutsu-tachi and patiently waited.

The lunar illumination enabled objects to be seen clearly within a distance of ten yards; beyond that, although things were still perceptible, the shadows could play tricks on you. So, despite his best efforts to pierce the darkness, Rikki-Tikki-Tavi remained ignorant of the identity of the creature until it was almost upon him.

"May the Spirit preserve us," the Warrior involunartarily whispered, his eyes widening in disbelief, when he finally realized the nature of the threat.

The thing was a giant spider.

Rikki whipped his prized katana from its scabbard and tossed the scabbard aside, the thirty-seven-inch-long sword gleaming, the razor-sharp blade reflecting the moonlight. This katana, the only genuine samurai sword the Family possessed, was Rikki's by virtue of his martial arts mastery. Among the hundreds of thousands of books in the Family library, volumes carefully selected by the founder of the Home, Kurt Carpenter, were dozens of books on unarmed combat and various disciplines in the martial arts, the majority of which were written by a man named Bruce Tegner. The Family Warriors spent years being instructed by one of the Elders, a former Warrior, in karate, kung fu, jujitsu, savate, and diverse other styles of martial combat. Of the twelve Warriors, one had displayed exceptional skill and outstanding ability while taking the Tegner classes, as they became known. This Warrior had later selected, from the hundreds of weapons stocked in the Family armory, an ancient katana as his principal weapon. He would relinquish it upon his death.

The spider paused seven yards away.

Rikki held his katana in both hands and raised the sword to chest height, the blade vertical, his powerful arm and shoulder muscles tensed. He had fought mutates before, many times, but never one of the rarer giants. As with the mutates, no one knew whether it was a consequence of protracted exposure to enhanced radiation levels, or a genetic imbalance triggered by one of the chemicals employed during the Big Blast, but cases of giantism occurred regularly. Five years before, four Family hunters, out after elk, encountered a giant wasp and were nearly killed. Inexplicably, the strains of giantism only appeared in insects or their close kin.

Like arachnids.

The spider, a six-foot-tall aberration of nature, moved several feet closer.

Rikki knew he'd seen this type of spider before, at its proper size, and he noted the features, trying to place it. The thing was black, with an extended, almost spherical abdomen, and two prominent jaw-like appendages. Its spindly legs, like the bulk of the body, seemed to possess a strange shiny quality.

Abruptly, Rikki remembered.

Just one spider, to his knowledge, had a strange shininess to its color.

The black widow Spider.

The black widow suddenly came at him, its jaws quivering, its toxic venom dripping from pronounced fangs.

Rikki couldn't repress a shudder as the thing closed in. He waited until the last possible instant and swung the katana, the blade biting deep, raking the black widow its eyes. He darted aside, to the left, swinging again, aiming at the cephalothorax, the front section of the spider, expecting an immediate kill. Instead, the blade deflected off the rock-hard carapace, the protective covering over the cephalothorax.

The black widow, despite its size, or perhaps because of it, was slower than a widow of normal size would be. It turned after the human, the fangs working expectantly.

Rikki backed away, searching for a weakness. He knew the arachnid was divided into three basic parts: the cephalothorax, the front portion; then a tiny waist, the pedicel; and finally the extended abdomen. Familiarity with the flora and fauna was extensively taught in the Family school. With the decline of humankind after the Big Blast, the wildlife had surged to unbelievable numbers, reclaiming the land for its own. Knowing the habits and dispositions of the varied creatures became indispensable to the Family's continued survival.

So how could he dispatch this menace?

The katana arcing downward, Rikki jumped in close to the widow, going for one of the rear legs. The meticulously forged blade did its work this time, completely severing the leg at its joint, a putrid liquid substance spurting over the ground. Before he could try for another appendage, the black widow hurtled sideways, its massive body slamming into Rikki and sending him sprawling. The jolt of the impact dislodged the katana from his fingers, the sword sliding a foot from his outstretched arms.

The black widow kept coming, its fangs snapping at Rikki's feet.

Rikki rolled aside, avoiding the Widow's mouth, lunging for his katana, and missing.

The black widow pushed itself forward, actually hopping, and landed on Rikki's legs, pinning him to the earth.

Rikki was on his right side, his frantic fingers inches from the sword.

The black widow paused.

"Can't say much for your dancing partners, pard," said a deep voice, and Hickok came into view, running around the spider and stopping near

Rikki. His Pythons were in his hands, cocked. "Don't move!" he ordered. "I'll try and lead it away."

"Save yourself!" Rikki urged, still striving to reach his katana.

"Be serious," Hickok grinned. "If you're hungry, gruesome, try eating these!" he said to the spider, pulling both triggers, the barrels pointed at the row of eyes above the mouth.

The black widow lurched, recoiling in pain, and heaved itself at this new danger.

"What's wrong?" Hickok laughed. "Lead not to your liking?" He backed away from the arachnid, intending to provide Rikki with a chance to grab his sword. "Come on, ugly!" he taunted the horror.

"Don't stand there!" Rikki shouted, finally free of the spider's weight. He scooped up his katana and leaped to his feet. "Kill it!"

"No need to fret, pard," Hickok chuckled, still backpedaling. "This is a piece of cake."

He tripped.

"Hickok!" Rikki yelled in alarm.

The black widow was eight feet from the gunman, an implacable killing machine, undeterred by its injuries.

Hickok, flat on his back, raised his Colts and fired at the eyes, again and again, one gun after another.

The black widow staggererd but didn't stop.

"Hickok! Move!" Rikki was in motion, running to the rear of the widow, his katana held over his head. He put every muscle in his body into a downward slash, uttering his kiai as he swung, the blade cutting like a hot knife through wax, cleaving the back of the abdomen in two.

The widow reared up and spun.

"Go for the eyes!" Hickok directed while reloading his Colts.

Rikki-Tikki-Tavi obeyed, slicing his blade from one end of the row of eyes to the other.

In agony, the black widow thrashed and squirmed, one of its front legs catching Rikki in the chest and knocking him down.

"Don't move!" someone commanded, followed by the booming of a shotgun, one shot after another, the buckshot blasting great chunks out of the spider's face, spraying the grass with pieces of the spider's flesh and a pungent sticky substance.

The firing finally stopped, and Rikki could detect a ringing in his ears. He looked down at his clothes, both his tattered jeans and his faded brown shirt, and grimaced at the gunk covering his body.

The black widow was lying on the ground, its body shaking uncontrollably, its face a ruined shambles.

Hickok walked over to Rikki, his Colts trained on the quaking spider. "Think it's dead?" he asked uncertainly.

"Nothing could live through that barrage," Rikki commented, rising. "Who . . . ?"

"Just little old me," stated a stocky, black-haired man wearing a green shirt and pants made from an old canvas. His brown eyes twinkled as he approached, a Browning B-80 automatic shotgun cradled across his brawny chest. "I heard some shots and came running. Lucky for you I didn't decide to have a snack on the way."

"We were doing okay without your help," Hickok said.

"White idiot speak with forked tongue," the newcomer gravely intoned. "Geronimo know better."

"I'd like to have seen you fight this thing, using the weapons we have," Hickok stated, peeved.

Geronimo, the only Family member with an Indian inheritance in his blood, grinned. "You went about it all the wrong way," he said. "Anyone could see that."

"And just how would you have killed this thing?" Hickok demanded. "Your tomahawks wouldn't of made a dent in it."

Rikki chuckled. Hickok and Geronimo were the best of friends, but they never seemed to tire of razzing one another. Their continual squabbling was common knowledge and a constant source of amusement; indeed, someone had once remarked that the day they ceased teasing each other would be the day the world came to an end.

"I would have killed it the right way," Geronimo remarked.

"Right way?" Hickok snapped, falling for the bait. "What are you babbling about?"

Geronimo made a pretense of yawning. "Everyone knows there is only one way to kill a spider."

"How's that, smart butt?"

"Simple." Geronimo winked at Rikki. "You step on it."

2

"I think you have more muscles than anybody I've ever seen."

"I exercise a lot."

"My father was strong like you," the girl revealed. "He's dead now," she added sadly.

"Both my parents passed on long ago," the dark-headed Warrior informed her. "People die, Star. It's inevitable. Try not to get upset over dying."

"How can I help it, Blade?" Star asked, gazing up at him, her green eyes watering.

"The Family believes people pass on to a better place when they die," Blade explained. "Whenever you think of a departed love one, remember they're still alive, waiting for you to catch up, and keep in mind you'll be joining them someday. It makes the sorrow of being separated slightly more bearable."

"I understand," Star said, considering his words. She studied the Warrior, marveling at his superbly conditioned physique. He was wearing moccasins and brown pants, the latter sewn together from an old tent. Two Bowie knives hung from his waist, one on each hip. An automatic rested under each arm, suspended in a shoulder holster.

"What are those?" she asked him.

"Vegas," Blade replied.

"And how did you get those?" Star inquired, pointing at the scars covering his broad chest, visible despite his dark tan.

Blade frowned. "You certainly ask a lot of questions."

"Rainbow says you never learn things unless you ask," Star said, gazing at the Block in which her mother was recuperating.

Kurt Carpenter, the wealthy filmmaker and survivalist, was responsible for the design of the Home. Carpenter had firmly believed World War Three was inevitable and, as with everything else he did, he had acted upon those beliefs. He had planned and built the Home, invited selected friends to the site when the world situation deteriorated to the critical point, and waited for the final folly. He had carefully picked the Home site, located far from any primary military and civilian targets, in northwestern Minnesota, on the outskirts of the Lake Bronson State Park.

The Home was watered by a large stream, entering the walls at the northwest corner and exiting at the southeast. Inside the compound, the stream was channeled along the base of the walls, forming a protective moat. The eastern half of the Home was devoted to agriculture and preserved in its natural state. In the center of the thirty-acre plot were the cabins, the living quarters for the married couples and their families. The western section contained the reinforced concrete Blocks, arranged in a triangular fashion, and devoted to specific functions. The armory was contained in A Block, B Block was the sleeping quarters for single Family members, the infirmary was C Block, D Block was their workshop area, E Block was the library, and F Block was devoted to farming and gardening purposes. Below each Block was a survival chamber for emergencies. Each of the Blocks, beginning with A Block at the southern tip of the triangle, was positioned precisely one hundred yards from the other.

Blade and Star were standing in the open area in the center of all the Blocks. Family members were everywhere, engaged in their daily activities.

"Do you think my mom will be all right?" Star asked Blade.

"You were there," Blade reminded her. "You heard the Healers. Your mother developed pneumonia. She's very sick, but with time and care she'll recover. You can visit her anytime you want. Don't worry. Our Healers are very good at what they do."

"I noticed," Star stated, "you all have . . ." She paused, trying to find the right word.

"Titles," Blade finished her sentence for her.

"That's it!" Star beamed. "How come?"

"The man who built this place wanted us to give titles to everyone. He said it gives a person dignity and self-respect." Blade stretched, his arms bulging, testing his strength, determining if he was fully recovered from the infection. He seemed to be.

"Some of my people have titles," Star began, then quickly stopped.

"What's the matter?" Blade grinned, the corners of his gray eyes crinkling. "Afraid you'll give us a clue as to where you came from? You've been here two days and haven't said a word. Why?"

"I'm sorry," Star apologized, "but my mother told me I'm never to let anyone know. You'll have to ask her."

"Which might be a while," Blade commented.

"She's still unconscious, and the Healers say she won't be up to a conversation for at least a week. Doesn't matter, though. You're both welcome here, for as long as you want to stay."

"Look!" Star pointed, excited. "Here come your friends."

Hickok and Geronimo approached from the direction of E Block, located at the northeastern apex of the triangle.

"So how's my princess today?" Hickok asked, sweeping Star into his arms.

"How did . . ." Star blurted, appearing startled. She recovered her composure immediately and giggled, hugging the gunman.

"Want to go see your mother?" Hickok asked.

"Can we?"

"You bet," Hickok assured her. "Let's go." He smiled at Blade and strolled toward C Block, Star laughing and pulling on his long hair.

"He's a new man," Blade remarked. "I'm glad that girl came along. His disposition has improved tremendously."

"Did you know Star and her mother are Indians?" Geronimo asked.

"Star told you that?"

"No. But Plato says they have all the classic characteristics, whatever that means. And here I thought I was the last one." Geronimo stared after Hickok and the girl. His brow furrowed.

"Maybe you'll find an Indian maiden and bind," Blade said, smirking.

"Wouldn't that be something," Geronimo responded, taking the idea seriously.

"We'll have a double wedding," Blade stated. "Jenny and I, and your maiden and you."

Geronimo noticed the huge grin on Blade's face. "Before I scalp you, I'm supposed to pass on a message from Plato. He wants to see you."

"I can imagine why," Blade commented, some-what ruefully.

"We've been back from Fox a month," Geronimo stated. "He needs us to go to the Twin Cities as he originally planned, before the Trolls attacked."

"Where is he?" Blade inquired.

"In front of E Block," Geronimo replied. "Fuss-ing over the SEAL. I swear he treats that vehicle as if it were his child."

"A lot is riding on that transport." Blade chuckled at his own pun. "You can't blame Plato for being anxious."

"How do you think Jenny will take your departure?" Geronimo asked, referring to Blade's intended.

"That worries me," Blade admitted. "After the Fox run, she's been more concerned about my safe-ty than before."

"You could remain here," Geronimo proposed. "We'll take Rikki along instead."

"And break up his Triad?" Blade shook his head. "Plato decided Alpha Triad should be the one to go, and we're going to be. Besides, who has as much driving experience as I do?"

"No one," Geronimo answered. "Although Hickok does have some, if you can call what he did driving."

Blade laughed. "I better see Plato. You coming?"

"Like to, but Plato also wants me to find Joshua. Catch you later." Geronimo ambled toward a stand of trees growing near A Block, one of Joshua's favorite places for meditating and worshiping.

Blade casually walked in the direction of the library, enjoying the warmth of the sun on his skin, relishing the feeling of being healthy again. He thoroughly detested the forced confinement imposed on him because of the infection. The

Healers, his darling Jenny one of them, had refused to brook any argument and compelled him to remain in bed until they were satisfied as to his recovery. Thank the Spirit the illness had waited to strike until they'd returned from Fox, the head-quarters of the Trolls! He spotted Cindy and Tyson, the brother and sister who were living an uncertain nomadic existence until the Alpha Triad had found them and brought them to the Home. They had adjusted quickly, and now appeared to be happy and contented.

One of the Gamma Warriors was on guard duty, pacing the rampart above the drawbridge. He saw Blade and waved.

Blade recognized the balding head and fancy blue uniform of Napolean, the leader of Gamma Triad. Napoleon had found an old Air Force uniform in the storeroom of clothes and material the Family maintained in the rear of B Block, sewn the holes and patched the rips and tears, and added silver buttons and a bright red sash. Hickok referred to Napoleon as "the Family dandy," a reference Napoleon strongly resented. Once, during a lighthearted social period around a fire, Hickok made a joke about Napoleon's style of dress. Blade recalled being shocked by the intense expression of hatred momentarily flickering across Napoleon's face. He remembered Napoleon had even reached for the Taurus revolver he wore, then stopped, evidently realizing drawing on Hickok was certain suicide. But why had Napolean reacted so violently to a harmless jest?

Blade's reverie was interrupted by the sight of the SEAL.

SEAL was an acronym for Solar Energized Amphibious or Land Recreational Vehicle, a prototype Kurt Carpenter had expended millions developing. After its construction, Carpenter had hidden the vehicle in an underground chamber. In a diary he had left behind, Carpenter advised his followers to avoid contacting the outside world for as long as possible. He had known society would revert to bestial levels after the War, and had wanted to protect his Family. Carpenter also had realized the Family would require a very special mode of transport once it decided to venture any distance from the Home. The SEAL was his gift to subsequent generations, a revolutionary vehicle designed to withstand the rigors of travel in a landscape altered by the ravages of nuclear war.

The SEAL was powered by the sun, the light collected by two solar panels affixed to the roof of the vehicle. The energy was converted and stored in unique new batteries located in the lead-lined case under the transport. The scientists and engineers had assured Carpenter the SEAL would continue to function provided the battery casings and the solar panels were not damaged.

In appearance, the SEAL resembled pictures in some of the library books of vehicles calls vans. The floor was an impervious metal alloy, while the body, the entire shell, was composed of a shatterproof and heat-resistant plastic, fabricated especially to meet Carpenter's rigorous speci-fications. Four puncture-resistant tires, each four feet high and two feet wide, supported the transport.

There was no sign of Plato.

Blade stopped at the driver's door and peered inside through the open window. The body itself, a light shade of green, provided one-way viewing; those inside could see out but, for security reasons, anyone outside could not perceive the occupants.

"Plato?" Blade called, wondering where his wizened mentor could be.

"I thought I recognized the owner of those large

pedal extremities," said a voice from under the SEAL.

"Plato?" Blade knelt and peered under the vehicle.

"Thanks for responding so promptly." Plato grinned, his affection conveyed in his kindly blue eyes. The head of the Family viewed Blade as the son he never had. His long gray hair and beard were streaked with dirt and grime, as were his baggy pants, a tattered pair of jeans, and his loose-fitting brown shirt. "I've been checking the SEAL to insure operational integrity," Plato explained. He crawled from under the vehicle and slowly stood, his arthritic knees bothering him as he straightened.

"Is it all set to go?" Blade asked.

"Absolutely," Plato replied, whacking the side of the transport. "Fit as the proverbial fiddle. Unfortunately, though, I've failed to ascertain the function of the mysterious toggles."

Blade knew the switches Plato referred to. The SEAL's Operations Manual, although it contained explicit instructions on the procedural operation and functions of the vehicle, did not mention the purpose of the four toggle switches in the center of the dashboard. They were marked M, S, F, and R. "No problem," Blade told Plato. "We can get by without using them."

"Just be certain no one touches them until I discover their primary function," Plato advised.

"We won't," Blade assured him.

"You know the reason I requested to speak with you?" Plato asked, his tone turning somber.

"I imagine you want us to leave for the Twin Cities soon," Blade responded.

"Affirmative," Plato acknowledged. "Tomorrow morning."

"What?" Blade's face reflected his surprise. "So

soon?"

"The sooner the better," Plato stated.

"But it's such short notice," Blade protested. "Jenny will be extremely upset."

"Would you rather inform her a week before your departure," Plato said gently, "and have her moping and crying for a whole week instead of one night? Which would be easier on her emotionally?"

Blade frowned and stared at C Block. "I see your point," he admitted regretfully.

Plato placed his right hand on Blade's broad back. "I am truly sorry for the imposition and inconveniences, but you know our records indicate each generation is experiencing decreased life spans and suffering from a form of premature senility. *I* have it," Plato said softly, "and it's affecting my behavior. I ache, I get absent-minded, and at times I behave like a silly ass. We must find a cure, and we need certain medical and scientific supplies to do it. Minneapolis and St. Paul are the nearest major cities. We believe they were spared a direct hit, and have every reason to speculate they are still standing. A major metropolis might contain all of the equipment we need. The Twin Cities is our best bet. I'm aware of the great distance involved, some three-hundred-and-seventy-odd miles, but it is imperative Alpha Triad make the trip."

"I know all of this," Blade reminded Plato. "It's just that after what happened with the Trolls, I'm not mentally prepared to leave Jenny, to be separated from her again."

"None of you have revealed much concerning your trip to Fox," Plato commented.

Blade stared into the distance, watching a flock of starlings wing over the forest.

"Would you care to talk about it?" Plato said softly.

Blade shook his head.

"You came close, didn't you?" Plato asked.

"We came close," Blade confirmed, vivid memories of sharp teeth and slashing claws, of a shredded throat and a bloody woman Warrior filling his mind, haunting him with their intensity.

"I will never be able to express the full extent of my gratitude," Plato said, opting to change the subject, "for saving my dear wife. I had given her up for dead long ago."

"You have been happier than I can remember ever seeing you," Blade stated.

"You rejuvenated my life, and have filled my soul with soaring melodies of love and an inner feeling of contentment. I feel complete again," Plato declared, smiling broadly. He noted Blade's sad face. "There is another reason . . ." he blurted out, then paused.

"What is it?" Blade asked. He leaned against the SEAL.

Plato glanced around to insure they were alone. "You might be wondering why I'm stressing that you depart as rapidly as feasible."

"I thought you might give us more time to acquaint ourselves with the SEAL," Blade confessed.

"I'd prefer to," Plato confided. "The risks, however, are quite high."

"I don't follow you."

"I suspect," Plato said slowly, glancing around again, "someone might attempt to steal the SEAL."

"What?" Blade stood erect, his hands dropping to his Bowies.

Plato nodded. "I have reason to believe that several members of the Family are not satisfied with the status quo."

"Who?" Blade demanded.

"I can't say, just yet. I have suspicions, but lack concrete evidence. Until I gather the evidence, I must keep my suspicions to myself. Suffice it to say, I fear the SEAL will be stolen if we leave it here much longer. Even if we posted guards, they still might manage to take it. I can't allow that, which is why I'm sending you out as quickly as I can, to remove the temptation."

"Who do you suspect?" Blade asked, his voice a throaty growl. "Who endangers the Family?"

Plato shook his head. "I can't say just yet."

"Maybe we shouldn't leave," Blade suggested.

"If I believed the situation was critical, I wouldn't be sending you out," Plato said sharply. "The Family will be fine."

"I don't know . . ." Blade hedged. The idea that someone in the Family might be turning against the Family stunned him. "Can't you give me any clues?"

Plato shook his head. "No. Not now. After you return, I will provide complete details, if I still feel the situation warrants such action. Who knows? By the time the Alpha Triad returns, everything could be fine."

Blade decided to take a firm stand. The safety of the Family, of his loved ones, of Jenny, was at stake. "I'm sorry, Plato. I'm a Warrior. It is my duty and responsibility to insure the Family is protected from any threats, from without and within. You'll need to tell me more than you have, or the Alpha Triad will not be going anywhere."

Plato frowned. "I didn't anticipate you would adopt this recalcitrant attitude. Very well, without divulging names, I can reveal that three Family members have aroused my suspicions. Conversations among these three have been overheard by others. These three apparently believe that the Family has existed in isolation long enough, and they want us to leave the Home and seek contact with any other survivors of the war."

"Isn't that exactly what we're doing?" Blade interrupted. "By sending Hickok, Geronimo, and me out, I mean?"

Plato sighed, and his slender shoulders slumped. "I've only mentioned a portion of their discontent. They are also dissatisfied with certain Family practices and, specifically, with the caliber of Family leadership. They believe I'm too timid, lacking in resolve. They . . ." Plato stopped.

"Go on," Blade goaded him.

"They . . ." Plato paused, reluctant to continue.

"Go on," Blade said flatly.

"One of them was overheard stating he felt he would make a better leader than myself," Plato finished in a rush.

"A power-monger in the Family?" Blade hissed the words through clenched teeth.

"Possibly."

"Then it's settled. I'm not leaving."

"You must."

"No way. The Founder was quite clear about what should be done in a case like this. No one who craves power, for the sake of power, shall be permitted to remain in the Family." Blade was angrily scanning the compound. "Who is it?" he demanded.

"I can't reveal that."

"Why not?" Blade exploded, attracting the attention of several nearby Family members.

"I've already told you," Plato said quietly. "I lack substantial proof. Hearsay is not adequate evidence. Besides, even if we assume the worst possible scenario, they are still in the talking stage. It will be some time before they build themselves up to the point where they contemplate action of some sort. The departure of the Alpha Triad might even prevent any rebellion. They'll be as excited as the rest of us, eagerly awaiting your return, your report. After you have returned from the Twin Cities, then the malcontents might agitate matters. I believe we are safe until that point."

"I don't like it," Blade announced. "We're taking a big risk."

"I assure you there is no cause for alarm," Plato stressed. "Remember, the Family will still have the protection of the Beta, Gamma, and Omega Triads. Rikki-Tikki-Tavi will be in charge of security in your absence. We are well secured against any internal strife."

"I still don't like it," Blade reiterated.

"Do you accept my assessment of the situation?" Plato asked.

"I suppose so," Blade said reluctantly.

"Good." Plato smiled reassuringly. "Don't worry. The Family will be fine while you are gone."

Will it? Blade wondered. Would the Family still be safe and intact when the Alpha Triad returned? If the Alpha Triad returned! "I have a question for you," he said, a touch angrily.

"What is that?"

"Do you still want us to take Joshua along tomorrow?" Blade questioned.

"We have been through this several times." Plato sighed. "You know I do, and you know my reason."

"You don't appreciate what it's like out there," Blade argued. "It's no place for a man devoted to spiritual concepts of peace and love, a man who won't kill under any circumstances."

"I want Joshua along for exactly that purpose," Plato stated. "Joshua is the Family's peace emissary, our good-will ambassador. Some of you Warriors are prone to shooting first and talking later. We need someone to extend the hand of friendship to any strangers you encounter on your run to the Twin Cities."

Blade shook his head. "I still don't agree with you," he said, emphasizing his position, "and neither does Hickok. Geronimo hasn't said how he feels about it." He shrugged his muscular shoulders. "What's the use . . ." he said, turning. "I need to clear my head."

Plato watched Blade shuffle off. The youth was obviously averse to leaving for the Twin Cities, and Plato couldn't blame him. "Poor Blade," Plato mused aloud. " 'You are the most immediate to our throne, and with no less nobility of love than that which dearest father bears his son do I impart toward you,' " he quoted from Shakespeare, one of his favorite writers.

Frowning, Plato climbed into the SEAL to insure all of their supplies—the food, ammunition, medical necessities, and other items—were stocked on board the transport. The interior of the SEAL was spacious. Two comfortable bucket seats provided seating in the front, divided by a brown console. Another long seat ran the width of the vehicle behind the bucket seats. In the back of the SEAL was a storage area, piled with provisions. In a recessed compartment under this section were two spare tires and tools they might need. Underneath the dashboard hung a red lever. Plato leaned over and moved it to the right. According to the Operations Manual, this lever activated the solar collector system. In the morning, a gauge above the red lever would indicate a full charge. The energization process required an hour on a sunny day.

Plato stepped from the transport and popped the hood, going over the engine, determining if all the parts were mechanically sound. Next he clambered onto the roof and inspected the solar panels.

Finally he crawled under the SEAL again and examined the batteries and their casings.

"Everything appears to be in order," Plato said to himself. He emerged from under the vehicle and stood, rubbing his dirty hands on his clothes. Tomorrow, the Alpha Triad and Joshua would depart on a trip destined to decide the fate of the Family. What would that fate be? he reflected.

Life?

Or death?

3

The July sun was beating down mercilessly even at
this early hour. Climate had been drastically
affected by the Third World War. Immediately
after the War, the atmosphere had become choked
with radioactive debris, dust, and smoke. Within
five years, most of this had dispersed. Now, a
century later, the sky was near normal, and the
Temperate Zones still enjoyed the passing of
seasons, but with a difference. The transitional
seasons, spring and autumn, were of shorter
duration than before the War. Summer and winter
were dramatically altered, characterized by an
extreme latitude of temperature fluctuation.
Summers were suffocatingly hotter, and the
winters were icily colder. Thunderstorms could
attain a staggering, raging intensity. Periodically,
inexplicably, every winter, pink snow would
descend.

The Family was gathered for the departure.

"It's going to be another hot one," Blade commented as he, Hickok, Geronimo, and Joshua approached.

Plato wiped the back of his right hand across his
sweating brow. "Indeed. How was your repast?"

"It was a good feed, old-timer." Hickok patted his stomach. "I'm going to miss the grub around here."

"You'll return to partake again," Plato said.

"Bet your boots!" Hickok pointed at the SEAL. "This contraption ready to go?"

"The SEAL is fully functional," Plato replied. "The only exceptions are those switches on the dash. As I advised Blade, you must not tamper with them until we discover their purpose. It is most peculiar they are not included in the Operations Manual."

"Don't fret yourself," Hickok suggested. "We managed to get to Fox and back without using them."

"Before you depart, there is something I must say." Plato stared earnestly at each of them in turn. "Believe me, if any other option were available, I would not be advocating this venture. If you only knew how often I have prayed there were another recourse available . . ." He let the thought trail off.

"The Spirit will guide us," Joshua assured him. Joshua was attired for the trip in faded beige pants and a brown shirt. He wore a gold chain and large cross around his neck. His brown hair, grown long, draped across his shoulders. He adorned his face with a full beard and moustache. His brown eyes, even his every facial feature, reflected an inner, sublime serenity.

Plato knew the identity of Joshua's childhood hero, and he understand why the sixteen-year-old Robert had adopted Joshua at his Naming. "Do you think I should call the trip off?" he asked, racked with doubts.

"No," Blade immediately answered.

"You don't?" Plato needed further assurance.

"The Family is depending on us," Blade stated.

"Whether we personally like it or not, we're committed. We can't turn back now, before we've even begun." He paused and locked his gray eyes on Plato. "After all, we don't want to be accused of timid leadership, now do we?"

Only Plato realized the significance of the statement, and he averted his gaze. Wasn't this ironic? he mentally told himself. Yesterday, Blade had wanted to call the Twin Cities Run off. Now, *he* did. When it came right down to it, he simply couldn't bear the thought of one member of his precious Family, the people he viewed as his cherished children, coming to any harm.

"Then it's settled," Hickok said. "Which is fine by me. I'm looking forward to a little action."

"If this trip is anything like the Troll affair," Geronimo cracked, "you'll get more action than you can handle."

Hickok patted the Pythons. "Wouldn't have it any other way, pard."

"The SEAL is loaded with all the supplies you should require," Plato remarked. "Do you have your weapons?"

"I refuse to bear arms," Joshua answered quickly.

"We have our weapons," Blade replied, speaking for the Warriors. His Commando Arms carbine was in the rear of the SEAL, along with Geronimo's Browning B-80 automatic shotgun and Hickok's Navy Arms Henry. The Family armory, in A Block, contained hundreds of weapons, a diverse assortment personally stocked by Kurt Carpenter. Carpenter had known his followers would need all the firepower they could muster if they were to endure, to survive in the shambles of civilization remaining after World War Three. He had overseen the stacking of crate after crate of the appropriate ammunition, and had included the equipment necessary for reloading and repair.

In addition to the Bowies on his hips and the Vegas in the shoulder holster, Blade carried two daggers, one strapped to his left wrist, another to his right calf. Three Solingen throwing knives, in a small leather sheath, were attached to his belt in the small of his back, hidden by the green shirt he wore. A folding Buck knife was in his right front pocket.

Hickok, as always, wore his Colts. In a miniature brown holster affixed to his right wrist, under his buckskin sleeve, was a two-shot Mitchell's Derringer. Tied above his left ankle was a four-shot C.O.P., in .357 caliber.

Geronimo carried the fewest weapons. An Arminius .357 was in a shoulder holster under his right arm. A pair of genuine Apache tomahawks, his favorite weapons, were angled under his belt, near the buckle.

"There is ample space if you want to take more," Plato mentioned.

"We have all we'll need. We should get going," Blade said.

"At last!" Hickok walked around the transport to the passenger side.

"But first . . ." Blade scanned the dozens of faces and spotted Jenny. She was standing forlornly under a nearby tree. "I'll be right back," he informed the others and moved through the crowd to reach her side.

Her blue eyes were watering, her cheeks streaked with her tears, and her beautiful blond hair was disheveled. "I don't know if I can take this," she informed him.

"We've been all through this," Blade reminded her, his eyes feasting on her loveliness. He wanted to brand this moment in his memory, to remember everything from the pout of her full red lips to her form-fitting buckskin breeches, even the contours of the white blouse she had sewn together from pieces of a torn sheet.

Jenny hugged him and pressed her left cheek against his chest. "Oh, Blade! I've dreaded this moment! I don't want you to go!"

"Please, Jenny, don't," Blade said, his voice husky. "It only makes it worse on us."

"I'm sorry," she managed to say. "I can't help myself." She buried her face and began sobbing.

Blade let her cry, uninterrupted. He twisted his neck and saw Joshua saying goodbye to his parents. How fortunate Joshua was to have his parents alive and well. None of the Alpha Triad had parents to worry about. Blade realized he was thankful his parents had passed on. If they were still with the Family, he doubted he would be able to depart. Leaving Jenny was hard enough, requiring every iota of his concentration and will power.

"I'm holding you to your promise," she said, looking up at him with tears running down her face. "We marry when you return."

"I meant it from my heart," Blade whispered. "I'll be counting the days until we're together again."

Jenny managed a smile. "I can't wait to bind with you."

Blade leaned down and kissed her passionately, forcefully. She clung to him in emotional desperation, her nails digging into his superbly muscled arms.

"Jenny," he began when they broke their kiss, "I want to tell you something. Remember these words when the nights are long and lonely. I love you with the depth and breadth of my soul. You mean more to me than life itself. I will be back to bind to you. Nothing, absolutely nothing, will keep me from getting back here. No matter how long it takes, or whatever obstacles I must overcome, I will return. And while I'm gone, every moment of every day, I will cherish your love for me in the core of my being."

Blade kissed her again, lingering, reluctant to part. Her heart was pounding in her chest, her fingers trembling.

Jenny gently withdrew her lips from his. She sniffled and smiled up at him. "I'm okay now. It's better if we don't drag this out any more than necessary. Let's join the others."

"You sure?"

"Positive."

Blade and Jenny slowly crossed to the SEAL, arm in arm.

Hickok, Joshua, and Geronimo were already inside the transport, Joshua and Geronimo in the back, Hickok sitting in the bucket seat on the passenger side.

"You can have more time to yourselves," Plato told them, feeling a profound wave of guilt over sending the Alpha Triad out into the world. What if they never came back?

"We're fine," Jenny said.

Plato's face was etched with sorrow.

"Believe me, we're fine." Jenny reached out and squeezed his right hand.

Blade, scanning the six dozen faces surrounding the SEAL, saw someone he needed to talk with. "Excuse me." He smiled at Jenny. "Be right back."

"Okay."

Blade made his way through the Family members until he reached Napoleon. "I need to talk to you," he told the Gamma Triad leader. "Alone."

Napoleon grinned, his balding head glistening in

the sun, and moved to one side, away from prying ears.

"What is it, Blade?"

"I want to warn you," Blade spoke quietly. "I talked with Rikki last night. He'll need your support while I'm away. Can I rely on you?"

"Need you ask?" Napoleon demanded testily. "But what do you have to warn me about?"

Blade glanced around them. "Plato has told me he suspects there is someone, maybe several members of the Family, who might cause trouble while Alpha Triad is away."

"Oh, really? Did Plato mention any names?" Napoleon inquired, his brown eyes darting nervously about.

"He wouldn't give me names," Blade replied. "But he has reason to believe that someone wants to be Family Leader."

"What?" Napoleon asked incredulously.

"That's right," Blade snapped. "A power-monger in the Family."

"I find that hard to believe," Napoleon remarked.

"Me too," Blade admitted. "The Founder was quite explicit in his diary. The Family must immediately expel anyone suspected of craving a position of power."

"I'm glad you let me know," Napoleon said, thanking him. "I'll keep my eyes peeled for you."

"I knew I could count on you."

"May the Spirit be with you," Napoleon said. "We'll all be looking forward to your return."

"Thanks." Blade shook hands with Napoleon and returned to the SEAL.

Napoleon watched him go. "And some of us," he said under his breath, "will be looking forward to your return with less enthusiasm than others."

Blade took Jenny's hand as the Family members

thronged the SEAL. Dozens came forward to offer
their best prayers and wishes for a safe trip. One of
them was Joshua's mother, Ruth.

"You'll watch out for my Joshua, won't you?"
she earnestly asked Blade.

"Of course we will," he assured her.

Ruth gazed at Joshua, tears rimming her green
eyes. "Bring him back to us, please," she beseeched Blade.

"Ruth, you'll see him again. Trust in the Spirit."

Ruth nodded and moved away.

The Alpha Triad's departure was a historic
occasion. Except for the Omega Triad on guard
duty, every Family member was at the SEAL.

Rikki-Tikki-Tavi came up to Blade. "Take care,
and don't fret over us." He would be in charge of
the Warriors with Alpha Triad gone. "Keep your
mind on the mission. May the Spirit smile on you."

Plato stepped in front of the SEAL and raised
his arms. "The time has come for the Alpha Triad
to leave us in quest of essential supplies and equipment we so desperately require. Much depends on
them. I know I speak for all of us when I proudly
say to these brave men that our love and prayers
go with them. We will be waiting eagerly for their
return. May the Spirit bless them on this enter-
prise."

Many members of the Family applauded and
shouted encouragement to the Alpha Triad
members and Joshua.

Plato walked over to Blade and Jenny. "The
keys are in the ignition," he said to Blade.

The two men gazed at one another, conveying
their affection and mutual respect in one glance.

Plato, impetuously, embraced Blade. "Take care,
son," he whispered.

Blade smiled. "I will." He turned and faced
Jenny.

"I love you," she said.

"I love you," he replied. He enfolded her in his arms. "Never forget that."

"Get going," she urged him, "before I begin bawling in front of everyone."

Blade stared into her eyes, holding her hand in his.

"Please, Blade, go." Her voice was breaking.

Blade climbed into the SEAL.

"At last," Hickok cracked. "I thought you were going to personally say so long to every member of the Family."

Blade ignored him. He suddenly felt an urge to get moving, to leave before he changed his mind.

Joshua waved to his parents, Ruth and Solomon. "I'll miss them terribly," he stated unhappily.

Blade twisted the key and the SEAL turned over. Those Family members standing in front of the vehicle moved aside.

"Try not to pull a Hickok," Geronimo advised.

"What's that supposed to mean?" Hickok rejoined. "I didn't do such a bad job of driving my first time out."

"No, you didn't." Geronimo chuckled. "If you conveniently forget trying to run over half the Family." He paused, grinning, then snapped his fingers. "Oh! And what about that tree jumping out in front of you and trying to wreck the transport?"

"Hey, pard," Hickok said, glancing over his left shoulder at Geronimo. "When you drive this critter, then you can talk."

Blade carefully pressed the accelerator and the SEAL moved forward. He saw Jenny waving, tears pouring from her eyes. Plato had his right arm around Jenny's shoulders. Blade shook himself and focused on his driving. Up ahead he

saw Brian, the Keeper of the drawbridge, assisted
by several other men, lowering the bridge, working
the massive mechanism, the system of gears and
pulleys, to the only exit from the Home.

"I can't believe it," Hickok exulted. "We're
finally on our way to the Twin Cities! Ya-hooo!"

"Does he often get this excitable?" Joshua asked
Geronimo.

"This is one of his calmer moments," Geronimo
answered.

The members of the Family were running after
the SEAL, many waving, the children laughing
delightedly, the majority of the adults ebullient.

"The adventure of a lifetime," Hickok said, his
face flushed, "and were on it! Who knows what
we'll find out there!"

Blade frowned. "I know what I'm leaving
behind," he said.

"You'll see her again," Hickok promised.

"How can you be certain?"

"I won't let anything happen to you, pard,"
Hickok assured his friend. The gunman playfully
smacked the dashboard. "Ya-hooo!" he shouted
again.

"You're certainly in a good mood," Blade commented. "Star has been a positive influence on you,
hasn't she?"

"That's part of it," Hickok agreed, grinning. He
wasn't ready to divulge the true motivation,
sparked by the incident the other night. He had
made a decision. After they returned from the
Twin Cities, he was going to track down the
remaining Trolls and avenge Joan's death. The
Trolls had removed his beloved from his life; he
would remove every last one of them from this
planet, and hopefully assuage his tormenting grief.
"Hi-yo Silver, away!" he happily yelled, pleased
at the thought of his eventual revenge.

"What in the world does that expression mean?" Joshua inquired.

"I read it in one of the western books in the library," Hickok explained.

"This promises to be an interesting trip," Joshua observed.

Blade, concentrating on driving the SEAL, bit his lower lip, thinking of Jenny. Had he made a mistake he would regret for the remainder of his life? Should he have stayed with the woman he loved? Would he ever see her beautiful face again? Clasp her in his arms? Hear her words of endearment? Hickok had said it best. Who knew what they would find out there?

4

Blade drove the SEAL at a sedate speed, still unsure of his ability and the SEAL's capability despite his previous experience on the run to Fox. He drove south after leaving the Home behind. They crossed rolling fields, following the guidelines Plato had prepared. A road atlas from the library was their means of navigation. Eight miles from the Home, as hoped for, they found Highway 11. Still passable, the road was cracked and riddled with holes. Portions of the surface had buckled over the years, with weeds growing in the exposed sections.

"We head west from here, right?" Blade asked, requesting confirmation.

Hickok, the map spread open on his lap, grinned. "Yep. West until we hit another highway, number 59 on this map. Later we cross over to Highway 10, and if I'm right, we'll then have smooth sailing into the Twin Cities."

"We hope," Geronimo threw in.

"Yeah." Hickok folded the map. "Where do you plan to stop for the night?" he asked Blade.

"Probably somewhere along Highway 59. We'll

get a good sleep, and begin the day early and refreshed," Blade responded. "What do you think?"

Hickok shrugged. "Makes no never mind to me."

"Wouldn't it be best to stay inside the SEAL tonight?" Geronimo offered.

"It would minimize the risks," Blade agreed.

"Risks, schmisks!" Hickok cracked. "I prefer to sleep outside, under the stars."

"Aren't you concerned that some creature might attack you in the dark?" Joshua asked.

"I can handle myself real good," Hickok stated confidently.

"It must be nice," Blade mentioned, slowly following the highway, avoiding the ruts and the potholes.

"What must be nice?" Hickok took the bait.

"To have your self-confidence," Blade said. "You know, I bet if you had your life to live all over again, you would still fall in love with yourself."

"That's not nice." Hickok looked hurt. "It's also not true. I'm one of the most modest people in our Family."

"What's that?" Joshua suddenly shouted, leaning forward, between Blade and Hickok, and pointing directly ahead.

Blade, startled, slammed on the brakes. The SEAL lurched and stopped.

Ahead, forty yards or so, in the center of the roadway, stood a large animal. It stood six feet high at the shoulder, and was nine feet in length. Huge, splayed antlers, longer and broader than any deer ever sported, topped a narrow, ungainly head. The creature was covered with brown fur, its legs long and hooved.

"What the blazes is that?" Hickok, astonished, asked.

"It's not an elk, is it?" Joshua was uncertain.

"No," Geronimo answered. "We've seen elk before."

"Think it's a mutation of some kind?" Hickok stared as the creature calmly stood its ground, casually munching on grass.

"I think it's called a moose," Geronimo ventured.

"I agree," Blade spoke up. "I've seen pictures of them in the Nature Series books. Funny, though. I didn't think their range extended to this area."

"According to the descriptions I read," Geronimo concurred, "their range doesn't."

"What do you make of it?" Hickok queried.

"I don't know," Blade said thoughtfully. "Maybe it was forced here by conditions elsewhere."

"What do you mean?" Hickok fidgeted in his seat. He could swear the thing was staring directly at him. Impossible, though. Nothing could see in from outside.

"Who knows what wildlife we'll encounter?" Blade replied. "The Big Blast undoubtedly destroyed wide tracts of land and probably caused massive animal migrations. Plato said we should expect to come across radiation zones, areas devoid of all life. The animals would avoid those areas, and would concentrate in the sections untouched by the explosions and the radiation."

"Maybe we'll meet a buffalo," Hickok joked.

"So how do we get around this moose?" Joshua inquired.

The vestige of the highway was passing through a densely wooded stretch, the trees pressing in on both sides.

"Should I shoot it?" Hickok suggested.

"No. We can't use the meat and we shouldn't waste the hide." Blade placed his chin in his hands and bent down, his elbows on the steering wheel.

A sharp, raucous sound pierced the air.

Everyone jumped, even the moose. It whirled and lumbered off into the trees.

"What the hell!" Hickok was grabbing for one of his Pythons.

Geronimo was glancing around, searching. "Where did that noise come from?"

Blade had involuntarily snapped backward. He eyed the dashboard. "I think it came from up here, somewhere."

"What was it?" Hickok demanded.

"Beats me," Blade admitted.

"Whatever it was," Joshua said, indicating the road ahead, "it got rid of the moose."

"Maybe this thing did it," Hickok suggested.

"What?" came from Geronimo.

"Sure. Maybe the SEAL did it, all by itself!"

"Be serious." Blade tenatively touched the steering wheel.

"I'm dead serious, pard," Hickok said, excited. "Maybe the SEAL scared off that critter."

"This vehicle can't think," Blade reminded him.

"How do we know?"

"Plato told us. He said some vehicles before the Blast were outfitted with something called a computer. These computers could think, could even talk to people. Carpenter probably didn't include a computer in the SEAL because he had reservations over whether his descendants could use one. Computers were complicated."

"And this thing isn't?" Hickok snorted.

"You needed special schooling to operate a computer," Blade said, furthering his case. "You also needed training to fix one if it broke. Computers died with the Big Blast. Whatever caused that noise wasn't a computer. One of us must have done something to cause it."

"I don't know," Hickok said doubtfully, not convinced. "I still think this thing can think for itself."

"Too bad it can't drive itself," Geronimo interjected.

Blade smiled and resumed their trip.

"You know," Hickok remarked after an interval of silence, "I've been thinking . . ."

"Uh-oh!" Geronimo promptly interrupted. "Now we're in real trouble."

" . . . and I've come to the conclusion," Hickok continued, overlooking the wisecrack, "we could run into just about any kind of animal the further south we go."

"Figured that out all by yourself, did you?" Geronimo smirked.

"It's really beginning to dawn on me," Hickok said seriously, "the magnitude of this experience."

"Magnitude?" Geronimo exploded in laughter. "I didn't think you knew a big word like that!"

"I was taught in the same Family school you were," Hickok reminded him. "We had the same teachers."

"Do you think any of these animals will pose a threat?" Joshua questioned.

"In case you hadn't noticed, Josh," Hickok replied, "we're surrounded by threats. There's mutates, and the clouds that eat you alive, and all kinds of critters just aching to chomp on you for a snack. Don't you realize how dangerous this mission is?"

"We'll just have to do the best we can," Blade said.

"Hope it's good enough," Hickok grumbled.

"The Spirit will guide us safely and enable us to overcome any obstacle," Joshua assured them.

Hickok twisted in his seat and faced Joshua. "I have something I want to say to you."

"There's no need," Blade interrupted, knowing

what Hickok was about to say.

"Yes, there is, pard," Hickok disagreed. "Listen, Josh . . ."

"Joshua," Joshua amended.

"Sure, Josh, sure," Hickok said, ignoring him. "I'm real glad you agreed to come with us on this here little trip, but I don't think it's the brightest idea you've ever had."

"Why's that?" Joshua asked quietly.

"This ain't the place for you," Hickok replied. "You belong back at the Home with the Family, teaching them about love and brotherhood and all that. You don't belong here with us. Josh, there's no telling what we'll come up against."

"As you said earlier about yourself," Joshua said, smiling at Hickok, "I can handle myself real good."

"Is that right?" Hickok bristled. "How?"

"What?"

"How the blazes are you going to handle yourself? What will you do if you're attacked? Will you defend yourself? You refused to carry a gun on this trip! Hell, man, you even refused to study Tegner."

While the Warriors were required to take the Tegner classes, using Bruce Tegner's books, each one filled with step-by-step diagrams and instructions and photographs of every movement and position, the martial-arts courses were optional for other Family members. Many elected to pursue the disciplines for other than combative objectives: some for health reasons, a few because of peer pressure, and others for a simple form of diversion. Whenever new classes were ready to begin, the individual members would be asked if they wanted to enroll. In recent years, one person had consistently refused to participate: Joshua.

"I have my reasons for not studying Tegner,"

Joshua said.

"I'd love to hear 'em," Hickok said, goading him.

"Will you leave him alone?" Blade took his eyes from the road for a moment to glare at Hickok.

"No," Hickok said stubbornly. "We should get this out in the open."

"This isn't necessary," Blade commented.

"It isn't?" Hickok retorted. "You're the one who spoke up against him coming along in the first place. You have a fair idea of what we can expect on this trip. Our lives are at stake. We need to know that the other person is going to back us up in critical situations. We need to know exactly where Joshua stands."

Blade opened his mouth to speak, then thought better of it.

"Okay, then." Hickok faced Joshua again. "Now that the objections are disposed of, let's get to the point. Can we rely on you, Josh? Will you back us up in a pinch?"

"I'm not certain how to answer that," Joshua replied.

"A yes or no would be nice," Hickok suggested.

"If only it were that easy," Joshua began, selecting his words carefully. "You want to know if I'll back you up in a crisis? The answer is yes, if the situation does not call for any active violence on my part. I . . ."

"No violence?" Hickok snapped angrily. "In case you haven't noticed yet, this is a violent world we live in."

"I have indeed noticed," Joshua responded patiently. "The world is full of madness and violence. It literally surrounds us. We're swimming in a sea of negative attitudes and reactions. You must come to appreciate my position."

"Which is?"

"I will not permit myself to become tainted by the insanity around me. I will not participate in a violent act. I will not kill a brother or sister, or a potential brother or sister. I will not allow the corruption outside to infect my inner state of being."

"Noble sentiments," Hickok stated. "I want you to be more specific. If we were attacked by a mutate, would you kill it to save us?"

Joshua's brow furrowed.

"Would you?"

"I'm thinking."

"Great. We'd be dead by the time you made up your mind to help." Hickok shook his head.

"I have never faced the situation you hypothesize," Joshua continued. "I would not want to see any of you harmed and would do whatever I could to aid you, short of killing the mutate."

"And just what the hell do you think a mutate would do to you?" Hickok exploded. "To any of us? They live for one reason, and one reason only. To kill! To kill anything and everything! It's their nature!"

"Their nature," Joshua agreed, "but not mine. Not ours."

"Men kill," Hickok growled. "Some men even like to kill."

"Men function on an animal level of existence, like the mutate does," Joshua agreed. "We must accept he truth of being children of the Spirit, and when we do we come to realize that this relationship makes every man and woman a spiritual brother and sister. We are all part of the same cosmic Family. The Spirit loves us all, equally. The Spirit is no respecter of persons. If we believe we are all children of the same Creator, how can we harm one another? The greatest commandment is to love the Spirit and one another."

"You're straying from the point," Hickok said testily. "We were talking about a damn mutate."

"Mutates must function according to their given natures. We must function according to ours. Mutates can not know the joy of communion with the Spirit. We can. Once we do, the experience changes us for all eternity. We are filled with a sense of wonder and happiness. Our souls are at peace. The idea of hurting another being becomes morally and spiritually repugnant."

"In other words," Hickok said, jumping in when Joshua paused, "we can't rely on you when the chips are down."

"I didn't say that."

"You sure as hell did, Josh. You sure as hell did."

They rode in uncomfortable silence until Blade detected a change ahead. "Look!" he urged them.

Highway 11 came to an abrupt end twenty yards ahead. Their path was blocked by a huge, steep trench, at least thirty feet across and equally as deep, with nearly vertical sides.

"What the blazes caused that?" Hickok questioned.

"It's been there a while," Geronimo noted. "Look at the vegetation in it, the grass and weeds and even some small trees."

"Maybe a flash flood washed it out," Blade speculated.

"It appears almost man-made," Joshua commented absently.

"Do we try to go through it?" Hickok inquired.

"Let's get a closer look." Blade drove the transport to the very edge of the gully.

"Blast!" Hickok snapped. "Those sides drop straight down."

"I can't risk it," Blade announced. "We could end up damaging the SEAL. We'll have to go around it.''

"Head north a ways," Hickok suggested. "It can't be that long."

Seven miles later, Geronimo leaned over Hickok's seat. "Don't you get tired of being right all the time?"

"There?" Joshua exclaimed, pointing.

A section of the trench had collapsed, providing a natural bridge. Without hesitation, Blade crossed over. He glanced north, observing the gully continued until it was out of sight. The SEAL plowed through a wall of weeds and he applied the brakes.

"Highway 59!" Hickok stated, excited. "We found it!"

As with Highway 11, a century of abandoned neglect had taken a toll. Potholes pitted the surface. Erosion had produced cracks and etched crazy cobweblike designs everywhere. Despite the wear and tear, sufficient roadway existed to permit the SEAL to navigate.

"All the roads must be in the same shape," Blade said thoughtfully. "Not exactly perfect, but we'll make better time than if we had to travel cross-country."

"Do you want to stop now or keep going for a spell?" Hickok asked.

The sun was directly overhead.

"Unless one of you objects," Blade responded, "I see no reason to stop for a midday meal."

"All right!" Hickok slapped his right thigh.

Blade turned the transport toward the southeast, toward the Twin Cities. He drove faster, a bit more confident. The engine purred flawlessly.

"I wonder how many days it will take us to reach the Twin Cities?" Hickok was studying the Atlas. "If we run into any more of those trenches, it will take us forever."

"Did you hear something?" Geronimo inquired. He cocked his head to one side, listening.

"Just the sound of the SEAL," Hickok answered, still looking at the map of Minnesota.

"No, not that," Geronimo said emphatically. "Something else, something nearby."

"I didn't hear anything," Blade said, agreeing with Hickok. "You sure you heard something?"

"Positive," Geronimo confirmed.

"Maybe it was that moose," Hickok said, grinning, "belching."

"What did it sound like?" Blade asked Geronimo.

"Can't be sure." Geronimo frowned. "Almost like the sound of the SEAL starting, only louder."

Hickok laughed. "I think you're cracking, pard. Tain't another motorized vehicle within a thousand miles of here."

Hickok was wrong. Again.

It came on them from the rear, abruptly bursting from cover in a tall clump of bushes, the driver gunning the engine as it cleared a small hump at the western edge of the highway. Chrome flashed in the brilliant sun, the spokes gleaming as the tires dug into the earth.

Blade, glancing in the rear-view mirror, spotted it first. "Behind us!" he shouted in warning.

It was already alongside the SEAL, the driver holding something dark and metallic in his right hand, pointing it at the SEAL.

"He's packin'," Hickok yelled, and ducked as the other driver fired at point-blank range, directly at Hickok's closed window.

They heard the thud and the whine as the bullet struck the SEAL and was deflected by the bullet-proof plastic.

The driver raced ahead, pulling away.

"A motorcycle," Blade answered, flooring the

accelerator.

The SEAL surged forward.

"We'll never catch him," Geronimo observed.

The motorcycle was clearly outdistancing them.

Blade kept the pedal on the floor, concentrating on the highway, trying to avoid the deeper potholes. The speedometer indicated eighty and climbing, and still they were falling behind.

"Hickok," Blade ordered, "drop him."

Hickok twisted in his seat. "Quick!" he said to Geronimo.

Geronimo turned and reached into the rear section. The Commando, Browning, and Henry were lying on top of the supplies piled in the back. He grabbed the Henry and passed it to Hickok.

"What are you doing?" Joshua asked.

Blade brought the SEAL to a stop, turning the transport, angling it across the road, Hickok's side to the fleeing motorcycle.

Hickok hastily rolled down his window and raised his Henry, sighting carefully.

"You can't!" Joshua exclaimed.

"He tried to kill us!" Blade reminded Joshua.

"Not in the back!" Joshua protested.

"We have no choice!" Blade declared, watching the other driver speed off. If Hickok didn't fire soon, even he wouldn't be able to make the shot.

"No!" Joshua shouted, flinging himself forward, lunging for Hickok.

Geronimo reacted instantly, clutching Joshua, restraining him.

"No!" Joshua struggled to break free. "He's another human being!"

"Not any more," Hickok said softly. He inhaled, held the breath, and squeezed the trigger.

"No!" Joshua screamed.

The motorcycle driver had just glanced back to determine his distance from the SEAL. They saw his head buck sideways, his arms jerking upward, his body falling to one side.

"Got ya!" Hickok was elated.

The driver tumbled to the ground as the motorcycle skidded, out of control, hitting a rut in the highway and flipping end over end for fifty yards before coming to a rest, a tangled, shattered wreck in the middle of the road.

Blade pulled out. "Good shot," he said to Hickok.

Hickok was grinning. "Piece of cake!"

"You shot him," Joshua said, stunned, going limp in Geronimo's arms.

Hickok glanced at Joshua. "I told you," he snapped, "you shouldn't have come."

"You just killed a man in cold blood," Joshua kept on, scarcely believing what he'd just seen.

"He tried to do the same to me," Hickok retorted. "What'd you want me to do? Wish him better luck next time?"

Blade braked and stopped the SEAL next to the driver. He turned off the SEAL and jumped out.

Hickok did likewise, training his Henry on the prone form.

Their attacker was lying on his stomach, a growing pool of blood forming under his head. He was tall, had black hair.

Blade slowly rolled the body over.

The man was young, maybe twenty-five or thirty. He was dressed in a gray shirt and jeans, neither of which showed any sign of prolonged wear. His hair was worn in a ponytail, tied at the shoulder with a length of string. Hickok's shot had caught him between the eyes, creating a good-sized hole, oozing blood. The back of his head, where the slug exited, was a total mess.

"Oh, dear Father!" Joshua and Geronimo had joined them. Joshua's face was pale, his expression horror-struck. He gaped at the puddle of blood. "Dear Father!" he repeated.

"Haven't you ever seen anyone shot before?" Hickok asked.

Joshua shook his head.

"What about that scavenger?" Hickok inquired. The ragtag scavengers had attacked the Home in the middle of the night. Someone had taken a shot at a Warrior sentry on duty on top of the wall. The shot had missed, the Warrior had sounded the alarm, and the Warriors and the unknown assailants had exchanged sporadic gunfire. The Warriors, and the rest of the Family, were left unscathed by the engagement, but the other side had suffered one casualty. A man was found lying behind a tree the next morning, shot through the chest. His clothes were in tatters, his physical condition emaciated. Everyone assumed the Home had been assaulted by a group of scavengers. "And how about the Trolls? Where the blazes were you during that fight? There were bodies all over the place," Hickok stated brusquely.

"I did not see any of the bodies," Joshua replied quietly, beginning to regain his composure.

"I'll check the cycle," Geronimo offered, and jogged off.

"Why'd he come at us?" Hickok questioned.

"I wish I knew," Blade answered, standing. He ran his left hand through his dark hair, reflecting. Why had this joker jumped them? What had he hoped to gain? Where had he obtained the motorcycle? Where was he from? There were a hundred unanswered questions, and he didn't like not having the answers.

"Should we bury him?" Joshua asked.

"What?" Hickok laughed. "I don't know about you, but I don't make a habit of burying people who try to kill me."

Blade knelt again, searching the dead man's pockets. In the left front pocket he found a handful of circular metal pieces.

"What are those?" Hickok leaned closer.

Blade studied them in the fading light. "I think they're coins," he speculated.

"Money?" Hickok said, shocked. "The guy is carrying money?"

"Appears so." Blade handed the coins to Hickok. He reached into the right front pocket of the jeans and found a piece of paper.

"Now what?" Hickok knelt alongside Blade.

Blade unfolded the piece of paper. It contained a crude, handwritten map. "We'll study this later." He folded the map and placed it in his own right pocket.

"Hey!" Hickok suddenly remembered something. "Where's his gun?"

"I haven't seen it," Joshua replied, glancing around.

Hickok stood and scanned the road and the surrounding area. He spotted a dark object lying in some grass at the side of the highway. "There!" He pointed.

"Where?" Joshua still hadn't seen it.

Hickok walked over and picked the weapon up, examining it. "Look at this!" He waved the gun at Blade. "A Ruger Redhawk! A .44-Magnum, six-shot, stainless-steel," he said in admiration. "Nice piece of hardware. I've seen it in the Gun Digest, but we don't have one at the Home."

"What have you got there?" Geronimo returned, carrying a leather pouch.

"His gun." Hickok showed the firearm to Geronimo. "What have you got?"

"The cycle is a complete loss," Geronimo said to Blade. "I found this lying ten yards from the wreck. Apparently, it fell off the bike. I've looked inside. It contains ammuntion and a folding knife." Geronimo paused, smiling. "And this." He held up a small object in his right hand.

"What's that?" Hickok moved closer.

"A box of matches."

"What?" Blade rose and took the box.

"New box." Geronimo beamed. "New matches."

"Can't be," Hickok stated.

"But it is," Blade confirmed, frowning. The box the wooden matches came in consisted of blank cardboard, devoid of any identifying marks. "It is."

"I thought it'd interest you," Geronimo admitted.

"See if these interest you." Hickok gave the coins to Geronimo.

"I don't believe it!" Geronimo exclaimed.

"This adds an entirely new dimension to our trip," Blade stated. He was uneasy, disturbed at discovering this stranger so close to the Home. Had the man been waiting for the SEAL?

"Doesn't it, though?" Hickok agreed. "I love a good mystery."

"What do we do now?" Geronimo inquired of Blade.

"We stay right where we are." Blade had already decided. "We'll spend the night in the SEAL . . ."

"Now wait a second, pard," Hickok said, beginning to protest.

Blade cut him off with a wave of his hand. "All of us will spend the night in the SEAL. It's the only cover we have, and this guy might have companions lurking about. It may be cramped, but at least we'll be alive in the morning. No one will be able to sneak up on us and slit our throats in the dark. Like it or not, it's the SEAL tonight."

Hickok shrugged his shoulder, indicating his acceptance.

"What about food?" Joshua spoke up. "Should I prepare a meal for us? I'm a good cook. At least, that's what I'm told."

"No fire tonight." Blade shook his head. "We've got some venison jerky in the SEAL and other provisions. A cold meal might not be the best, but it's the safest. Let's get inside and lock the doors."

"What about our departed brother?" Joshua asked, pointing at the motorcycle driver.

"He ain't my brother," Hickok retorted.

"All men are your spiritual brothers." Joshua looked Hickok in the eyes. "The Spirit gave each of us life and loves all of us equally. The Spirit is no respecter of persons."

"Men are," Hickok rejoined. "The Spirit may love us all, but men don't. Some men love you, some don't."

"Love is derived from understanding," Joshua said. "When we learn to understand one another, we will, in the process, grow to love one another."

Hickok sighed. "Can't you see it yet?" he asked, annoyed.

"See what?" Joshua asked, perplexed.

"When someone is trying to kill you, when they have a gun pointed at your head, you don't have much spare time to develop a mutual understanding. It's you or them. And I intend to insure that in each and every instance it's them and not me." Hickok pointed his Henry at the body. "Case in point."

Joshua quietly stared at the deceased driver. He shook his head, turned, and walked back to the SEAL.

"He's taking this hard," Geronimo observed.

"Serves him right," Hickok said testily. "He shouldn't be on this expedition."

"Plato had a reason for sending him with us." Blade joined their conversation. "We should leave him to his own thoughts tonight. I imagine he has a lot to meditate on. Besides, we have enough to keep us busy. Let's get inside."

"And the body?" Geronimo inquired.

"We leave it for the carrion-eaters," Blade responded.

"Joshua will be upset," Geronimo noted.

"Unfortunate, but it can't be helped. I know it's only noon or so, but I want to stay here the remainder of the afternoon and tonight. Let's see if anyone shows up. The biker's ambush was too calculated for my liking. He might have friends."

Blade drove the SEAL into a stand of trees and they settled in for the long vigil. The three Warriors remained awake until the early morning hours, discussing the ramifications of the attack. They ate a meal of venison jerky and water, their speculations continuing unabated. Why had they been attacked? Where was their attacker from? His clothing, possession, and the cycle all were relatively new. How was that possible? Did it mean that certain cities had been spared in the Big Blast? Were some industries still intact? Had the Family, isolated in a remote corner of the country, fallen out of step with the rest of civilization? Was the Family an outcast commune, out of touch with society? The three talked for hours, finally agreeing further consideration was senseless.

"We just don't have enough to go on," Hickok said, summing up their deliberations.

"Agreed. Until we do, it's useless to worry ourselves. What say we get some sleep and start off early?" Blade slouched in his seat, making himself comfortable.

"Good idea, pard." Hickok yawned. "I'm a mite bushed."

Geronimo leaned back, resting his head on the top of the seat. He too was weary. It had been an eventful day, and only their first on this trip. He glanced at Joshua, pitying him, imagining Joshua's turmoil. Joshua had not said a single word all night. He had sat with his elbows on his knees, his hands cupped together, his chin resting on his hands, his eyes closed, sorting his thoughts. He had even refused to eat. Geronimo flinched. One of the tomahawk handles was poking him in the side. He shifted position and aligned the handle to alleviate the pressure. The Arminius was snug under his right arm, his Browning behind him in the rear section of the SEAL. Good thing they had brought along the firepower. It appeared they'd be needing their armament, if today was any indication. One day out, one attacker dead. How many bodies would they rack up tomorrow? His last thought, before drifting into sleep, was to wonder if any of those bodies would be one of theirs.

5

Blade woke up to the sensation of a hand on his shoulder, shaking him. He opened his eyes, collecting his thoughts. "What is it?" he mumbled. The dead biker was where they had left him.

"You mentioned you wanted to start at first light," Joshua said, withdrawing his hand.

The sun was emerging over the eastern horizon.

"Thanks." Blade twisted in his seat, facing Joshua. "We were up so late, I might have overslept. Did you get any sleep?"

"No."

"You should have."

"I required time to commune with the Spirit," Joshua explained. "I wouldn't have been able to rest, even had I wanted to do so."

"Understand," Blade said, sighing. So much for his great idea. No one else had appeared during the night. "Let's wake the others."

"I'm awake," Geronimo said quietly, his eyes still closed. "Hickok kept snoring, kept waking me up. If we stay inside the SEAL tonight, can we muzzle him or nail his mouth shut?"

"I don't know," Blade joked. "It'd be too tempting to leave it that way in the morning."

"And you're supposed to be my friends?" Hickok sat up and stretched. "Pretty comfortable in here, wasn't it?"

"For some of us more than others," Geronimo stated.

"We're getting an early start today, aren't we?" Hickok stared at the pale gray sky. "Usually you don't start picking on poor helpless me until the sun's been up a couple of hours."

"You want a fire for breakfast?" Geronimo asked Blade.

"Not really," Blade replied. "Unless you do. I'd prefer to take off as soon as possible."

"Fine by me," Hickok said. "Just give us a moment."

"For what?"

Hickok opened the door. "This SEAL might be a mechanical marvel, but someone neglected to install a crucial part."

"Such as?" Blade remembered to throw the red lever.

Hickok gave Blade a searching look. "Your brain doesn't function so hot this early, does it? Want me to put a puddle on the floor before you get the idea?"

"Thanks just the same."

Hickok eased his body to the ground.

Geronimo leaned forward. "Hey, you be careful in those trees."

Hickok smiled. "I didn't know you cared that much."

"Just wouldn't want you to get bitten on the ass by a mutate when you pull down your pants. The poor thing might die of blood poisoning." Geronimo smirked.

Hickok made a show of rolling his eyes upward. "Why do I even bother?" He ambled off.

"He's got the right idea," Geronimo agreed, climbing out.

Everyone relieved himself, they consumed a meal of bread and water, and the second day's journey began.

"Any idea how far the first town will be?" Blade asked Hickok when they were finally under way, as they passed the dead biker.

"Won't know until I find out where we are on Highway 59," the gunman replied.

They rode in silent expectation. Blade acquired new assurance as he easily avoided ruts and holes in the road. At frequent intervals they would encounter sections of crumpled, buckled roadway, and Blade would make a brief detour along an adjacent field, rejoining the highway when its condition improved.

"Can I drive some today?" Hickok asked.

"Please, spare us!" Geronimo threw in. "I want to . . ." He paused, straining forward. "Look!"

Blade slowly applied the brakes, bringing the SEAL to a stop. A small, rusted sign stood at the side of the road. It read HALMA.

They were parked on a small rise. Below, the highway descended to a small town. Or, the remains of one. Even at a distance of a quarter mile, they could tell the buildings were in dilipidated shape.

"Think it's inhabited?" Joshua asked.

"We'll soon find out." Blade eased the transport ahead. "Everyone keep alert."

Geronimo passed out the long guns, handing Hickok his Henry and placing the Commando Arms Carbine on the console next to Blade. He picked up his Browning, insured it was loaded, and released the safety.

Joshua was apprehensively watching the proceedings.

Hickok bent over and picked up two items from the floor at his feet. "Here." He turned and gave the items to Joshua, who instinctively took them before he fully realized what they were.

The Ruger Redhawk and the leather pouch.

"What am I to do with these?" Joshua demanded, offended.

"Didn't you learn anything yesterday?" Hickok asked sadly.

Joshua dropped the gun and the ammunition pouch onto the floor. "I won't use a gun," he stated stiffly. " 'Thou shalt not kill,' " he quoted from Scripture.

"Suit yourself, pard," Hickok replied, frowning.

The SEAL was nearing the outskirts of Halma. At close range, they could see all of the buildings had sustained moderate damage. Roofs were blistered, partially gone in many instances. Walls were broken, cracked, and crumbling. Broken windows were everywhere.

"Think it got caught in the Big Blast?" Hickok speculated.

"Doubt it." Blade stopped the SEAL, mentally debating whether to drive into Halma or reconnoiter on foot. He opted for driving in. "Not enough destruction."

"Where'd everyone go?" Hickok asked.

"Who knows?" Blade drove forward, his nerves tense. "The Family records say that the government forced mass evacuations after the War. Maybe everyone had to leave."

Halma turned out to be completely deserted, all signs denoting it had not been inhabited for a long, long time. They stopped at the southern edge of town, pondering their next stop.

"What's the next town?" Blade asked.

"Hmmm." Hickok ran his index finger down the map. "Another small one called Karlstad. About five miles or so."

"Here we go." Blade gunned the SEAL.

Karlstad, situated at the junction of Highway 59

and 11, was another Halma, abandoned, in disrepair, obviously not used for years.

"Do you detect a trend here?" Hickok asked as they sat in the SEAL, parked in the center of town.

"Will every place we come to be like this?" Geronimo wondered.

Blade sighed. "So what's next?"

Next turned out to be Strandquist, seven miles south on Highway 59, exactly like Halma and Karlstad.

"This is depressing," Hickok commented. "I'm keyed for action, and we can't find a living soul in these parts."

"Don't forget the guy on the motorcycle," Blade reminded him. "He had to come from somewhere."

"Where? Mars?"

Eleven more miles brought them to a small community named Newfolden.

"This is becoming monotonous," Hickok cracked in disgust. "I'd hoped we'd fine someone by now. Where did the government evacuate everyone to anyway?"

"Somewhere in the southwest," Blade commented absently. Another ghost town? How many would they come across like this? "What's the next one?"

"You sure are a glutton for punishment." Hickok checked their location. "The next one was bigger at the time of the Big Blast. Had about ten thousand people. Known as Thief River Falls. Map shows a small regional airport. We're heading for the big time now!"

Blade drove on. "How many miles?"

"Seventeen."

The SEAL doggedly ate up the distance.

"Have you noticed," Geronimo observed at one point, "that we haven't seen much wildlife so far? A few birds, and a few miles back I spotted a herd of deer. That's been it."

"What's so strange about that?" Hickok asked.

"Just think of all the animals around the Home. I expected to find wildlife abundant here too. This area clearly escaped the brunt of the Big Blast. Why aren't there more animals?"

"Maybe the critters are afraid of this contraption." Hickok gave the dashboard a whack.

"Could be," Geronimo agreed, sounding doubtful.

Blade too had deliberated the same question. Geronimo was right. There should have been more wildlife. Were the animals avoiding the highway for some reason? Why would they do that? So many questions. So many unanswered questions.

"There! Up ahead!" Geronimo broke into his reflection.

Thief River Falls, two hundred yards distant, the first buildings visible around a small curve.

Blade braked the SEAL.

"Looks as run down as the others," Hickok mentioned.

Blade sighed. The few buildings he could see were shabby ruins, pitiful remnants of their former splendor.

"We're bound to encounter civilization sooner or later," Joshua chimed in optimistically.

Blade nodded grimly, driving ahead. The SEAL reached the outskirts of Thief River Falls.

"I've got a feeling . . ." Hickok levered the next round into the chamber of his Henry.

Blocks passed, building after broken building.

"Listen," Geronimo said quietly, leaning forward.

"I don't hear anything," Joshua stated.

Blade did. He stopped the transport.

"What the blazes is it?" Hickok asked, rolling down his window.

"Music," Geronimo suggested.

Blade rolled down his window. The Family owned over a dozen assorted musical instruments. Guitars, drums, a trumpet, trombone, and others. Those members with musical aptitude were encouraged to spend as much time as possible cultivating their talent. Many a night passed with the entire Family gathered to listen to one of its few remaining sources of entertainment.

These sounds were different. Music, yes, but harsher, more strident notes than any the Family instruments could produce.

"It's coming from up ahead," Geronimo said, "from the center of town."

Blade slowly drove the SEAL in the direction of the music.

"If we do find someone," Joshua said, "will you permit me to talk with them before you commence firing?" He was looking directly at Hickok.

"Maybe you should stay in the SEAL," Hickok replied. "There could be trouble."

"I was sent to act as mediator," Joshua reminded Hickok, his voice tinged with anger. "You can't hide me away every time we meet someone!"

"Safer for you," Hickok said, "safer for us if we do."

"There!" Geronimo pointed.

Blade stopped.

The center of Thief River Falls consisted of a profuse growth of trees, tall grass, and bushes.

"Must have been a park once," Hickok noted.

The buildings surrounding the former park were all shabby, unkempt, except for one. A two-story concrete structure, due south of the town square, displayed signs of recent maintenance. The walls were painted white, the front door still hanging on its hinges, and, unlike any other building in sight, this one had glass windows still intact. The raucous music was coming from this building, through several open windows.

"We're being watched!" Geronimo pointed again.

A stocky man, dressed in black, carrying a shotgun, was standing on the roof of the concrete structure, studying the SEAL. He suddenly whirled and disappeared from view.

"Don't like it," Hickok commented.

"What do we do?" Geronimo asked Blade.

Blade picked up the Commando and opened his door. "We go in. Hickok. Joshua. Myself. You stay with the SEAL. No one is to come near it, under any conditions."

Geronimo nodded his understanding.

"Do we have to take Josh?" Hickok demanded, climbing out. He alertly scanned their immediate vicinity.

Blade nodded.

"Why?"

"Plato gave us specific instructions. Joshua is right. He was appointed to act as our official Family mediator. We'll let him have his chance."

"And if they turn out to be hostile?" Hickok asked.

"You know what to do," Blade responded.

Joshua stood on the ground, stretching. "Thank you, Blade," he said, expressing his gratitude. "I won't let you down."

Blade motioned for Joshua to proceed. They cautiously approached the building.

The music abruptly ceased.

"They know they've got company," Hickok stated.

The front door opened. A lean man wearing jeans and a brown shirt, a revolver strapped around his narrow waist, stepped out, smiling, friendly.

"I don't trust him," Hickok whispered to Blade.

"Well, hello there!" The stranger walked down the front steps and extended his right hand. "It isn't often we get new faces around here. My name is Bert."

Blade and Hickok held back, tense, watching the building. Joshua looked at them, shook his head, and walked up to Bert.

"Greetings, brother." Joshua smiled. "We are happy to meet you."

Bert eyed Joshua quizzically. "Is that a fact?"

"Indeed," Joshua affirmed. "You are the first person we have . . . talked to . . . since our journey began. We are extremely pleased to meet you."

"Why don't you come inside and meet the others?" Bert asked. "You can bring your friend." He indicated Geronimo, who was now sitting in the front of the SEAL, leaning out the window, staring at them.

"Certainly." Joshua turned and waved, beckoning Geronimo to join them.

Geronimo glanced at Blade.

Blade shook his head. "He stays with our vehicle," he said to Bert.

"You worried someone might run off with that thing?" Bert laughed. "Ain't any scavengers in Thief River Falls. Only us."

"Convenient," Hickok commented.

For an instant, Bert's brown eyes narrowed. He grinned and placed his right hand on Joshua's shoulder. "Come on in."

"Thank you, brother."

"Brother? We aren't related."

They walked up the steps.

"All men are sons of the First Source and Universe Creator," Joshua said. "This cosmic truth makes all men spiritual brothers."

Bert gaped at Joshua in frank amazement. "Is

that a fact?" He smiled.

"It is a paramount universal truth," Joshua seriously intoned. He went to enter the building.

"Hold it," Blade directed. "Me first."

"Ain't very trusting, are you?" Bert stepped aside. "I don't think we've been introduced."

"Oh!" Joshua grinned sheepishly. "I forgot. I'm Joshua. This is Blade. And the one with the eyes that never stay still is called Hickok."

"Hickok." Bert said the name deliberately, arrogantly.

"You stay put," Blade ordered Joshua. He entered the building, immediately crouching and moving to the right, keeping his back to the wall, examining the room he found himself in.

The chamber was spacious, well lit by overhead lights.

They have a generator, Blade mentally noted.

There were four men in the room. Two were seated at a circular table in the center of the room, a deck of cards on top of the table. The cards were neatly stacked.

They aren't playing, Blade told himself. They just sat down, probably placed the cards there to make him believe they were enjoying a card game.

To the right of the men at the table, leaning against the railing to a flight of stairs, stood the third man, cradling a rifle in his arms. This one was short, bald, and obese.

The fourth man stood behind a bar running the length of the left side of the building. He was tall, broad at the shoulders, wearing his brown hair long. An automatic was on the bar top, within easy reach.

All four men were studying Blade.

"Howdy there, friend," one of the men at the card table greeted Blade. "No need for the hardware." He pointed at the Commando.

Blade slowly lowered the muzzle, his neck hairs prickling the back of his neck. Hickok was right. This setup stank. Still, he had to give them the benefit of the doubt. Ostensibly, they were sociable enough.

"You can come in," Blade announced for Joshua's benefit.

Joshua strolled into the room, all smiles, his hand reaching out for the big man at the table, the one who had spoken. "Hello. My name is Joshua. Thank you for welcoming us."

The big, bearded man smiled up at Joshua, his beady eyes narrowing slightly. "It isn't often we get strangers passing through. My name is Joe." He shook with Joshua and indicated an empty chair on the other side of the table. "Have a seat and we'll get you something to drink."

"Thank you." Joshua sat.

Blade frowned. Joshua had sat in a chair located between his position against the wall and the big man at the table, something a trained Warrior would never do. His line of fire was blocked. Pretending to be interested in surveying the room, he leisurely moved several paces to his right, insuring a clear shot at the two sitting at the table and the man leaning against the rail.

Hickok had walked in, directly up to the bar. He smiled at the man behind the counter, placed his Henry on the bar top, and rested his hands on the edge of the bar. His body was angled sideways, allowing him to keep his eyes on all four men. "I sure could use a drink, pard," he said to the barman. "You got any fresh milk?"

The barman laughed. "Milk?"

"Yep. Milk," Hickok answered, still smiling, his eyes gleaming.

"Sorry, sonny." The barman guffawed. "We ate our cow a while back."

"What do you have?" Hickok's hands lowered almost imperceptibly.

"The real article." The man reached under the bar and froze, his eyes widening.

Hickok's Pythons were pointed directly at his face.

"Whew! Did you see him draw?" Joe exclaimed. "Did you see him draw?"

"I saw," came from Bert. He was standing just inside the doorway, his right hand resting on his revolver.

"He's fast!" Joe glanced at Bert. "Maybe the fastest I've ever seen."

"Oh, I don't know," Bert remarked testily. "I know one person who could match him."

"Now who would that be?" Joe chuckled, baiting Bert.

"Hey, mister," the barman said to Hickok. "I ain't reaching for a gun."

"Bring your hand up slow," Hickok stated through clenched teeth. "Real slow."

The barman complied, raising a bottle and gently placing it on the bar. "This is what I was getting. You wanted something to drink, remember?"

Hickok relaxed a bit. He twirled his Colts and slid them into their holsters. "What is that stuff?"

"Whiskey. Top grade too."

"Whiskey? I've never had it. What's it like?"

The barman gaped at Hickok. "Never had whiskey? Where you from, sonny? Another planet?"

Hickok didn't answer.

Joshua cleared his throat. "You'll have to forgive my impetuous friend," he said to Joe. "He evidently enjoys demonstrating his skill with firearms every opportunity he gets."

"Really?" Joe thoughtfully replied. He quickly

glanced at Bert, then his eyes darted toward Hickok.

Blade was the only one who caught the motion. He watched out of the corner of his left eye and saw Bert move four steps to his left, still holding the butt of his revolver. Bert was now directly behind Hickok, about twenty feet away, out of Hickok's range of vision. Blade knew they were setting themselves, biding their time. He abruptly realized the man they had seen on the roof was not in the room. Where was he? Upstairs? Outside, stalking Geronimo? Geronimo could take care of himself. They had five men in this room to deal with.

"So," the man called Joe said to Joshua, "Where you boys from?"

Joshua opened his mouth to answer, but Blade cut him off. "Here and there."

Joe gazed at Blade. "Don't mean to be nosy!" He spread his large hands on the table. "Just trying to start conversation, is all. I take it that Sammy didn't send you?"

"Sammy?" Joshua repeated, puzzled. "Who is Sammy?"

"The big man," Joe said solemnly. "Top dog. What Sammy says goes."

"Where does this Sammy live?" Joshua asked.

"South of here a ways. We do some trading with Sammy from time to time. Run errands when Sammy needs it. Things like that."

"We don't have a Sammy in our Family," Joshua said. "At least, I don't think we do."

"You must have one hell of a big family if you don't even know everyone who's in it!" Joe laughed.

"Is there anyone else living in Thief River Falls?" Joshua politely inquired.

"Nope," Joe responded. "Just us. And we don't

actually live here. We're just staying here for a spell, sort of watching over things."

"You wouldn't know anyone who rides a motorcycle?" Joshua asked casually.

Joe attempted to disguise his reaction, but Blade noticed his features cloud for an instant.

"What's a motorcycle?" Joe innocently asked.

"A means of transport," Joshua answered.

"Like that thing you have outside?"

"The SEAL? It's quite different from a motorcycle."

"Never quite seen anything just like it," Joe said. He was inching his right hand under the table.

Blade noted the other man at the table already had both of his arms out of sight.

"Have you ever been to Minneapolis?" Joshua asked Joe.

Joe hesitated. "Once or twice," he finally replied. "Why?"

"That is our destination," Joshua said, displaying his inherent honesty.

"You don't want to go there."

"Why not?"

Joe shook his head. "Bad place. Bad. Violent types live there. Not friendly, like us."

"Violent?" Joshua asked, alarmed. "How do you mean?"

Joe leaned toward Joshua. "Sonny, they'll kill you quick as they see you. Believe me, you're safer staying away from Minneapolis. Say," he said, changing the subject, "are you hungry?"

"We could use some food," Joshua admitted.

Blade saw his chance. "We have provisions in our transport. Joshua, why don't you go get some for us?"

"No need for that." Joe's right hand paused at the table's edge.

"We have plenty," Blade mentioned.

"So do we," Joe protested. "Why don't you have some of ours?"

Blade smiled, his finger curling around the Commando trigger. "Wouldn't hear of it. You've been kind enough to us, so allow us to return the favor. Joshua, go get some food for us."

"But if they have some they're willing to share . . . " Joshua began.

"Do as I told you," Blade curtly ordered.

Joshua smiled at the other men, rose, and departed.

"He's a nice boy," Joe commented.

"None nicer," Blade admitted.

"I like 'em lean," Joe continued. "Great body." His right hand had disappeared under the table.

"I don't suppose you would be willing to raise your hands over your heads while we disarm you?" Blade tensed, ready.

Joe laughed. "You got a great sense of humor, sonny. You know better."

"And if I said we'd leave now, without any fuss?" Blade offered them one last chance.

"Sorry." Joe shrugged his shoulders. "We have our orders."

"The one you called Sammy?"

"The same."

"What's he have against us? We don't even know him?"

"Sammy always has good reasons," Joe stated. "Don't know why, but Sammy says you guys must buy the farm. Nothing personal, you understand?"

"I understand."

"And don't you worry none," Joe said, grinning maliciously. "We won't harm that Joshua. I intend to take real good care of him. Real good care," he emphasized, licking his thick lips.

"Say, Joe?" Hickok interjected.

"Yeah?" Joe kept his eyes on Blade.

"Anyone ever tell you that you're one miserable

son of a bitch?''

The room exploded with deadly action.

Hickok's guns were up and he was turning, even as Bert managed to clear leather. The Pythons cracked and Bert slammed into the wall and crumpled to the floor.

Joe and the other man at the table were bringing their weapons to bear, Joe a revolver, the other man a sawed-off shotgun.

Blade crouched, swinging the Commando in an arc, the slugs ripping into Joe and the other one, their chests erupting in spurts of flesh and blood.

The barman had his hand on the automatic, trying to aim it, but too late.

Hickok's Pythons roared and the barman's eyes vanished, the back of his head bursting outward.

The man with the rifle was stupidly attempting to raise his rifle and sight at Blade.

The Commando cut him in two at the waist, doubling him over, toppling him to the floor.

"Not bad," Hickok said in the quiet that followed. "Five men in about four seconds. Omega Triad, eat your heart out!"

Feet pounded on the outside steps, and both men swung to cover the door.

Joshua ran in, holding a bag of food in his left hand, out of breath. "Dear Father, no!" He surveyed the carnage, stunned, his senses faltering. "No! No!"

Hickok moved from one fallen foe to another, rolling them over, face up, insuring they were finished.

"Why?" Joshua turned to Blade. "Why did you do this?" His voice was rising, cracking, strained with emotion.

"We had no choice, Joshua," Blade said quietly.

"Had no choice?" Joshua repeated, dazed.

"Besides," Hickok said, pausing next to Joshua, "I can't abide people who make fun of cows."

Joshua spun on Hickok, his face contorted. *"Make fun of cows?"* he shouted. He grabbed the front of Hickok's buckskin with his free hand. *"Don't you realize what you've done?"*

"Messed up the room a bit."

"You've killed five men, five sons of God!"

"Josh, I think you better calm down. You're starting to get hysterical." Hickok spoke gently.

Joshua released Hickok and slumped against the wall. His left foot slipped on something, and he glanced down at the floor, at a piece of human flesh lying in a puddle of blood.

"Joshua," Blade began, "I'm sorry, but . . ."

The blast of three shots, from a shotgun, from outside, stopped him short.

"Geronimo!" Hickok was already in motion, racing out the door.

Geronimo was standing over a prone figure lying behind bushes at the edge of the town park.

Hickok, Blade on his heels, raced up to him.

"You okay, pard?"

Geronimo nodded. He pointed his Browning at the man on the ground. "Tried to sneak up on me. Imagine that! A whitey trying to sneak up on a red man! That's like a cat trying to teach a dog to bark."

"It's the one from the roof." Blade recognized him.

"I heard the shots inside and was coming to help," Geronimo explained, "when he popped up and let loose. His shot was hasty. He missed. I didn't."

"Yuck." Hickok grimaced. "That Browning sure did a number on his face."

"What face?" Blade asked.

Geronimo hefted the Browning. "This thing's something! It's like carrying a portable cannon."

"Knew you'd like it when I picked it for you." Hickok beamed.

"Where's Joshua?" Geronimo wanted to know.

Blade and Hickok realized Joshua had not joined them.

"We better get back to him," Hickok stated.

Blade put his hand on Hickok's arm. "Let me have a few moments alone with him."

"We should secure the area," Hickok reminded him.

"You two stand guard outside," Blade directed. "Let me have some time with Joshua, then we'll sweep."

"Old Josh did look a little bent out of shape," Hickok agreed.

"I'm beginning to have my doubts about the wisdom of Plato sending Joshua on this trip," Geronimo confided to his friends.

"If he's going to get upset every time we kill someone," Hickok added, "he'll spend this entire trip miserable."

Blade went inside.

Joshua was sitting at the table, his face in his arms, weeping.

Blade walked up to him and put his right hand on Joshua's shoulder. "Feel like talking?"

Joshua spoke without looking up. "I don't know if I can take much more of this."

"You can take it."

"Do you realize," Joshua said, sniffing, "in two days you have killed six men?"

"Seven," Blade reluctantly corrected.

"Geronimo shot one outside?"

"Yes."

"Seven brothers shot dead in two days," Joshua said bitterly. "That must be a new Warrior record."

"We don't like killing, Joshua, any more than you do."

Joshua lifted his tear-streaked face. "How can

you say that, Blade? I would never kill another son or daughter of the Spirit."

"They were planning to kill us."

"They told you that?" Joshua demanded.

"Not in so many words. Their actions gave them away."

"I didn't notice anything!"

"You weren't looking." Blade paused, searching for the right words. "Joshua, you only look for the best in everyone, and you completely overlook the worst. Those men were planning to catch us off guard and kill us in cold blood. Could we allow that to happen? What would the Family do without the supplies we're supposed to get? It was either them of us."

"Maybe we could have talked to them, reasoned with them," Joshua protested. "Surely there was something we could do?"

Blade shook his head.

"But we're required to love one another! Not kill. 'Thou shalt not kill,' " he quoted again from the Bible.

Blade sighed. "Joshua, what would you have us do? Should we have let them kill us? Not resisted? Submit without a fight? What would that prove?"

"I don't know," Joshua said sadly. "I just don't know anymore. I'm so confused."

Blade recalled a quote. "Didn't the Master tell us not to cast our pearls at swine, or something like that?"

Joshua thought a moment. " 'Give not that which is holy unto the dogs, neither cast ye your pearls before swine, lest they trample them under their feet, and turn again and rend you.' "

"Wouldn't that apply in this case?"

Joshua was struggling to regain his shattered composure. "I don't know, Blade. I apologize if my behavior disturbs you. I never expected this to happen. I thought friendliness and love would prevail in every contact we made."

"Is that being realistic?"

"I need time to reflect," Joshua said to himself.

Blade squeezed Joshua's shoulder. "I recognize the past two days have been a shock to your system, to your soul. There's no need for you to apologize. We'll bear with you for as long as it takes. If it's any consolation, I thought you did a real nice job."

"I did?"

"Sure. You were as open and friendly to these guys as you could possibly be. The fault for what happened doesn't lie with you."

"Where does it lie?"

"When you find out," Blade replied, "would you let me know?"

"I'll commune with the Spirit, see if I can perceive an answer."

"Good. Now we've got work to do. You sit here for as long as you need."

Joshua stood. "I'm ready to assist in any capacity you require."

Blade smiled. "Good." He walked to the door and motioned for the others.

Hickok glanced at Joshua as he entered. "You okay, Josh?"

Joshua nodded.

"How do you want this handled?" Geronimo asked Blade.

"You stay outside with the SEAL," Blade instructed him. "We can't afford to have anything happen to it. Keep your eyes open."

"Eyes like a hawk." Geronimo grinned, and left.

"And me?" Hickok inquired, hefting his Henry.

"There's a door over there," Blade pointed at the far corner of the room to their left. "See where it goes. I'll check upstairs."

"Be careful."

"You too."

"Piece of cake."

Hickok made for the door.

"What about me?" Joshua asked.

Blade frowned. "I hate to ask you to do this," he said, " but would you collect their firearms and place them on the table?"

"I can do that."

"And if you feel up to it," Blade continued, wondering if, perhaps, he was pushing Joshua too far, "could you pile the bodies near the doorway?"

Joshua's face paled. "As Hickok says," he answered gamely, "it would be a piece of cake."

Blade stepped over the dead man at the base of the stairs and climbed to the second floor. Three doors, all closed, fronted a narrow hallway. He moved quietly to the first door, twisted the knob, and pushed it open, the Commando ready, just in case. The first room contained stacked boxes. Blade examined them and discovered spare ammunition and dozens of cans of food. The mystery deepened. The labels on the cans were all fresh, printed not too long ago. Where had these men obtained them?

The second room was their sleeping quarters. Four worn mattresses were arranged on the floor, piles of discarded clothes strewn in random fashion. The room reeked of body odor. You certainly couldn't say much for their housekeeping.

Blade stopped at the third and final door. He pressed his left ear against the wood, listening. Had he heard a faint sound? There it was again! Soft, almost a moan.

Hickok came into view at the top of the stairs.

Blade placed a finger over his lips, cautioning Hickok to exercise discretion. He jerked his thumb at the door.

Hickok nodded and padded forward, the Henry

tight in his grip.

Blade waited until Hickok was standing to one side of the door. He caught Hickok's eye, nodded, and threw the door open.

Both Warriors dropped to one knee, sweeping the room with their weapons, braced, prepared.

The guns weren't necessary.

A solitary mattress occupied the center of this room. The window was closed, the shade drawn, the air stale and rank, worse than the second room.

"We'll I'll be!" was all Hickok could manage to crack.

The sole occupant of the room was a young woman. She was tied, spread-eagle, on top of the mattress, her hands and ankles firmly secured to nails inbedded in the floor. Her mouth was gagged with a wad of dirty cloth. She was stark naked, her muscular body covered with welts and open sores, cuts and scrapes.

"She's been beaten, bad," Blade said, stating the obvious.

"She's black!" Hickok exclaimed, marveling. The Family initially had had a black couple, long since dead.

They stood and approached her.

The woman's brown eyes widened in apparent fear, and she feebly struggled against her bonds.

"Doesn't look like she's eaten anything in a long time," Blade said, noticing her flat stomach, her skin tight against her ribs. Her skin wasn't truly black; it was a light dusky shade.

Hickok knelt near her head. "Hey, lady, don't worry none. My pard and I will get you out of here."

The woman stopped struggling and stared at them, confused.

Blade drew his right Bowie.

Her eyes opened even farther, and she renewed her efforts to break loose.

Hickok placed a hand on her sweaty brow. "Relax, dummy. I said we're not going to harm a hair on your head." He touched her hair. "Will you look at this? It's all curly! Never saw hair like this before."

The woman suddenly began choking, her body racked by violent spasms.

"Quick!" Blade urged. He cut the two ropes holding her ankles.

Hickok placed his Henry on the floor and pulled the gag from her mouth. She began taking deep breaths, her body shaking.

Blade sliced the ropes attached to her wrists.

"Take it easy!" Hickok put his hands under her shoulders and began to lift. "We'll get you some water."

The woman unexpectedly twisted and bounced to her knees, displaying surprising strength, scrambling to one side, grabbing the Henry and leveling the rifle at Hickok before they could stop her.

"Now wait a . . ." Hickok began.

She shoved the barrel up to his face. "One move, sucker, and I snuff your honky ass!"

Hickok grinned. "Will you give me the gun?"

"I mean it, white meat!" she warned, her voice rising.

"I believe you do, ma'am." Hickok sat down, laughing.

The woman kept looking from Hickok to Blade, unsure of herself.

"We won't harm you," Blade assured her.

"How can I be sure of that?" she asked, trying to rise. Her legs were too weak, and she sank to her knees again.

"If we were going to kill you," Hickok stated flatly, "you'd be dead by now. We wouldn't have bothered untying you."

"You're not one of the Watchers?" she

demanded.

"What's a Watcher?" Hickok asked her.

"Don't jive me, honky! Everybody knows about the Watchers. They stay outside, keeping an eye on us, stopping any who try to get out. They caught me." She suddenly stopped, weaving, the barrel of the Henry dropping.

"Were the men who were here some of these Watchers?"

"Yeah." She glanced at the doorway. "Where are they? I heard shooting."

"We killed them," Hickok informed her.

She studied Hickok's face. "I bet you're good at killing, ain't you, white boy?"

"I think so," Hickok said confidently.

"You really ain't going to kill me?" she asked incredulously.

"Not until you put some clothes on." Hickok grinned.

For the first time she became conscious of her appearance. "You sure are a strange one, white meat. Don't matter none, anyhow." Her voice was becoming weaker. "I couldn't stop you. Need food," she mumbled. "Need rest. So tired. So damn tired." She slipped forward, fainting.

Hickok caught her and lowered her to the mattress. "She's sure got a lot of spunk, doesn't she?"

Blade was on his feet. "Sure does. Stay here. I'll get Joshua." He ran off.

Hickok ran his fingers through the woman's Afro. "You sort of remind me of someone," he told the unconscious form. He folded her arms across her breasts. "Someone I was quite fond of. Her name was Joan," he said sadly. "She was a beautiful woman."

The gunman sat with his legs crossed, thoughtfully staring at the woman, waiting for his friends.

"Well, I'll be damned," he said at last.

6

The late afternoon shadows were lengthening across the park outside, covering the SEAL, which was now parked directly in front of the concrete building, securely locked for the night. A strong breeze rustled the trees in the park.

Inside, under the overhead lights, Blade, Geronimo, and Hickok sat at the card table, finishing their meal.

"Think she'll be all right?" Hickok asked.

"Joshua said she would," Blade reminded him.

"That's the fourth time you've asked the same question," Geronimo said, grinning. "I wish I had someone to worry over me the way you worry over her."

"She's a good kid," Hickok retorted stiffly.

"Some kid." Geronimo swallowed a mouthful of water from his canteen. "They must believe in ample . . . physiques . . . where she comes from."

"Let's take stock," Blade said, interrupting their banter. "We have some important items to consider. The men we killed today, these Watchers, wanted us dead. Why? Where were they from? For that matter, where is the girl from?"

"She'll tell us once she wakes up," Hickok said.

"I hope so."

Geronimo leaned back in his chair. "I keep wondering where they got all of that stuff." He stared at the pile of personal possessions he had collected from the dead men, heaped on top of the bar counter. "Knives, coins, keys, a compass, and all the rest. None of which show the slightest indication of age. Who were those guys?"

"That reminds me." Blade leaned forward. "Where are those guys? I never thanked you for disposing of the bodies. Did you bury them?"

"In a manner of speaking. I found a hole in the middle of the road, about two blocks from here. A heavy metal cover was lying to one side of the hole. Don't know where it led, but I dumped the bodies down it."

"A hole?" Blade repeated, mystified. "Freshly dug?"

"Nothing like that," Geronimo stated. "Made from concrete, I think. Some type of access tunnel under the street."

"Tunnels under the streets?" Hickok said, alarmed. "Why would they have tunnels under the streets? Could these tunnels be inhabited?"

"Doubt it." Geronimo shook his head. "I didn't detect any signs of life."

"We'll investigate one of these tunnels if we get the opportunity," Blade commented. "Let's get back to these Watchers. One of them mentioned they were following the orders of someone called Sammy. Remember?"

"Yep," Hickok affirmed. "Why?"

"Look at these." Blade reached into his pocket, withdrew three coins, and dropped them on the table.

"Where'd you get these?" Geronimo asked.

"One from the guy on the motorcycle, the other

two from these men."

Hickok was studying the coins. "They're all the same!"

"Look at the inscriptions," Blade suggested.

"They each have the likeness of a bearded man wearing a funny hat on one side," Hickok said, flipping the coins over. "On the other side they have a large one or a five or a ten."

"What does it say about the numbers?" Blade asked.

" 'In the Name of Samuel,' " Hickok read aloud. "Say! Hold the fort! Isn't Sammy short for Samuel?"

"It is," Blade confirmed.

"You think there's a connection?" Geronimo inquired.

"It would seem to be the obvious conclusion."

Hickok scratched his forehead. "So who's this Samuel?"

"Wish I knew." Blade reached into his other pants pocket. "There's more. While Geronimo was getting rid of the Watchers and you were helping Joshua minister to the girl, I remembered the piece of paper we removed from the cyclist. See what you make of it." He gave the slip of paper to Geronimo.

Geronimo inspected the paper. "A handwritten map. A dot in the lower right corner, marked with a TRF. A line running from the dot and joining another line. Where they meet, there's a K written in. The second line runs at right angles to the first. Part way along it, just above, is a large circle. What do you think it all means?"

"Place the paper on the table," Blade directed, "with the dot facing south and the large circle toward the north."

Geronimo did as instructed. Hickok leaned over to get a better view.

"Good. Now what if that dot in the lower right,

with the TRF next to it, stands for Thief River Falls?'' Blade reached over and ran his finger along the lines. ''What if this first line is Highway 59? See this letter K, where the lines meet? Wasn't it at Karlstad we found the junction of Highway 59 and 11? If I'm right, wouldn't this second line stand for Highway 11? And if it is, what does that make the large circle?''

''The Home,'' Hickok whistled. ''I'm impressed.''

''I'm worried,'' Blade confided.

''Think that guy on the cycle was deliberately keeping an eye on the Home?'' Geronimo asked.

''It looks that way,'' Blade admitted. ''I suspect he was linked up, somehow, with the men here. The one called Joe showed a peculiar reaction when Joshua mentioned the motorcyclist.''

''Then the motorcyclist,'' Hickok deduced, ''was one of these guys. One of the Watchers.''

''Watching us,'' Blade agreed.

''So what's our next move?'' Geronimo questioned. ''Keep going to the Twin Cities or return to the Home?''

Blade leaned his chin on his right hand, his elbow on the table. ''I've given the matter serious consideration today. These Watchers, so far, have not done anything that would lead me to believe an attack on the Home was imminent. They do exactly what their name implies. Watch. On the other hand, Plato made it perfectly clear the Family requires additional supplies. I say we continue on to the Twin Cities and stock up, then get back to the Family.''

''What about the things we've confiscated here?'' Geronimo asked.

Blade sat back. ''We'll stash the weapons and the food and clothes in one of the other buildings, one that's deserted and has been for a long time. If more of these Watchers come here while we're in the Twin Cities, I doubt they would find the cache. We'll pick it up on our way back to the Home."

"What about that generator I found in the basement?" Hickok inquired. "And that music machine behind the bar counter?"

"I believe they were called stereos," Blade stated. "We'll dismantle the stereo from the bar, and carry the generator up from downstairs. We can hide them with the weapons and food. Plato had a generator on his list of supplies to obtain. This way, we won't need to pick one up in the Twin Cities. We can bring one back, though, if we find one. Two generators would be ever better for the Family. Any objections or other points to raise?"

"I think you've pretty well covered everything, pard," Hickok said.

"What about the girl?" Geronimo asked.

"She's awake," said a voice from the stairs.

They turned.

Joshua was standing on the third stair, his hands on the railing.

"Josh, I didn't know you could move so quietly," Hickok said, complimenting him. "We didn't even hear you. Have you been taking sneaky lessons from this red savage?" He nodded toward Geronimo.

"Despite what you might think, Brother Hickok," Joshua said, "there are a few things I do very well."

"You said the girl is awake?" Blade demanded.

"Yes. She has an amazingly strong constitution. She's apparently been beaten and tortured and sexually abused, but she hasn't complained." Joshua paused, frowning. "She may be suffering delusions, though."

"Why do you say that?" Blade rose from the chair.

"She keeps insisting on seeing someone called White Meat. I repeatedly told her there is no White Meat here."

Hickok stood, grinning. "Well, well, well. Yes, Josh, there is a White Meat here."

"You?"

"None other. I better go up and see her." Hickok started for the stairs.

"Do you need any help?" Geronimo smirked.

Hickok bounded up the stairs, ignoring the barb.

"We'll go up too," Blade said to Joshua. "I have some questions that girl is going to answer. Geronimo, stay down here and keep an eye open. Never know when more of the Watchers may turn up."

"Got it." Geronimo picked up his Browning and walked to the front door.

Blade led the way up the stairs, Joshua following, to the room the woman was in. Joshua carried his medicine bag in his left hand, the buckskin bag containing the medical supplies, the ointments and herbs and other organic remedies and aids prepared by the Family Healers.

The woman was laughing when they entered the room.

"Hey, honky," she said to Blade as he came in, "this bozo is something else! Know what I mean?"

"Now if we could just figure out what," Blade said, joking with her.

The woman was clothed with pants and a flannel shirt from the other room. Joshua had washed her, dressed her, and tended to her numerous wounds during the day. He'd also placed a blanket over her to keep her warm.

"How are you feeling?" Joshua asked her.

"Better," she admitted. "White Meat tells me I have you to thank for that."

"It was nothing," Joshua said modestly.

"Sure was, honey." She looked down at the blanket. "Most folks nowadays would have killed me outright, or put me to other uses, if you get my drift." She grinned. "Can't hardly believe my luck! Finding out there still are some nice people in this world. Men too! Don't that beat all! Even the Horns ain't as nice as you been to me."

"Can any man or woman do less when a brother and sister is in dire need?" Joshua asked. "We are all children of the Spirit. We must never forget this truth."

"Hey, you sure you ain't one of the Horns?"

"What is a Horn?" Joshua asked her.

"You never heard of the Horns?" She rose on her elbows, surprised.

"No."

"How about the Porns?"

Joshua shook his head.

"Where are you guys from anyhow?"

"We'll get to that in a moment," Blade interjected. "Are you hungry?"

"I could eat a whole dog," she conceded.

"I'll prepare some soup," Joshua offered. "We have canned food taken from the Watchers. Would that be okay?"

"It beats what they was feeding me."

"Which was?"

"Nothin'," she replied. "Unless you count what they was poking between my legs."

"I'll get that soup," Joshua said, blushing.

The woman laughed. "Look at him! He's turning red! I don't believe it!"

Joshua quickly departed.

The girl laid back down. "Whew! I'm dizzy! Better not push myself just yet."

"You take it easy," Hickok told her. "You've nothing to worry about with us around."

She gazed up at him, her eyes soft in the light

from a single bulb burning in a socket directly overhead.

"I'm sorry to do this." Blade sat down next to her. "We need to ask you some questions."

"I can handle it," she assured him. "Besides, I owe you. You saved my life."

"What's your name?" Blade began his questioning.

"Called Bertha. Most of my friends call me Big Bertha, on account of my boobs."

Hickok chuckled.

"Where are you from?" Blade asked her.

"From the Twins."

"The Twin Cities?" Blade inquired, excited.

"Some still call it that. Used to be called some other weird name before the War. Long, long time ago. Don't remember what it was."

"How'd you get here?" came from Hickok.

"Dumb luck, I guess." Bertha pouted, her lips forming a small *o*. "Z wanted me to scout west of the Twins . . ."

"Who is Z?" Blade broke in.

"Zahner. Our leader. We all just call him Z for short. He wanted someone to see if the Watchers cover every exit from the Twins. You see, everyone knows the Watchers are there. No one knows where they come from. They block every road out of the city, and they kill everyone who tries to get out. Don't know why. No one's tried to get past them in years."

"If you want to leave the city," Hickok said thoughtfully, "Why don't you just go overland, avoid the highways, and cut across country?"

Bertha snickered. "You crazy, White Meat? The Uglies will get you sure as I'm lying here!"

"Uglies?" Blade reflected a moment. "Could she mean the mutates?"

"Why don't you just shoot the Uglies?" Hickok asked her.

"Wish to hell I could! But guns in the Twins are scarce, and ammo even rarer. The Horns have a few, the Porns even more, and we got three. We need 'em to preserve our turf. Can't allow any guns to leave the Twins. Have you ever tried to stop an Ugly with a club or a knife? Ain't done, bro. The Uglies stay out of the city, and we stay out of the country."

"So this Z sent you to find a road that might be clear?" Blade goaded her.

Bertha sighed. "Yeah. Z thought that maybe, just maybe, the Watchers weren't covering all the roads. I went out 'bout two weeks ago on one of the small roads. Got twenty miles from the Twins and was caught by a Watcher patrol. They had their fun with me, and then passed me to another group of watchers. They got their jollies, and I was passed to this group in Thief River Falls. They weren't able to get their rocks off before you guys showed up." She reached out and placed her hand on Hickok's. "Thanks, White Meat. Sooner or later they was going to waste poor Bertha."

"Piece of cake," Hickok told her.

"Why did this Z want to find a way out of the city?" Blade inquired.

"Because we're tired of all the fighting."

"Fighting?"

"Yeah. The Porns attack the Horns, and the Horns go after the Porns, and they both try and get us whenever they can."

"Does your group have a name?"

"We're mainly called the Nomads, 'cause we don't give our allegiance to the Porns or the Horns. Then, of course, there's also the Lone Wolves, the ones that keep to themselves and prey on everybody else. That leaves only the Wacks."

"The Wacks?" Blade was striving to make some sense from all this information Bertha was supplying.

"The crazies, man, the crazies! You never want to get caught by the Wacks! They'd eat you alive."

"They're cannibals?" Hickok said, shocked.

"What's a cannibal?" she asked him.

"A cannibal is a person who eats other people," Blade answered her.

"Yep. Some of the Wacks have been known to munch on their captives. Just thinking about 'em gives me the creeps!"

"Do these groups," Blade inquired, trying to sort the facts, "fight among themselves all over the city?"

Bertha yawned. "No, man, no. The Porns, the Horns, and us all got our own turf we protect. The Wacks and the Lone Wolves attack you anywhere. The Wacks just pop up from the underground."

"Underground?"

"Yeah, They come up out of the manholes at night, lookin' for food and such."

Blade bit his lower lip, reflecting. All of this was completely alien to any of his past experience. What was he to make of it? How should it affect their trip to the Twin Cities?

"What's turf?" Hickok wanted to know.

Bertha studied him, perplexed. "You don't know what turf is? Where are you boys from, White Meat? Turf is our territory. The Porns have the western part of the Twins. The Wacks are based in the south. The Horns have the eastern part, and some of the north. Mainly, though, we hold most of the north. It's the smallest turf, but then they got more soldiers than we do."

"Soldiers?" Blade repeated, surprised. "You have armies?"

"Not the way I think you mean, man," Bertha answered. "A soldier is anyone who does fightin' for their side. Get it? I'm a soldier for the Nomads. One of their topnotch soldiers," she proudly boasted.

"I knew it." Hickok grinned.

"What do you fight about?" Blade asked her.

"Just about anything, honey." Bertha laughed. "We fight to protect our turf, and we fight to attack theirs, and we fight because we don't much like one another, and because we're all different. We don't believe in the same things."

"That's a reason for killing one another?" Blade placed his hands behind him and leaned back.

"Can you think of any better?"

"I'm sorry, Bertha," Blade told her. "I really don't understand any of this. I'm trying. I really am. But it doesn't make much sense. Can you comprehend any of this?" he asked Hickok.

"I wish. I see that these people are all trying to be top dog in the Twin Cities, but I don't know the reason they're fighting. Does anyone know?" He turned to Bertha. "Is there anyone who knows when and why all of this started?"

Bertha was thinking. "There might be one man. He's the oldest Nomad. Almost forty years old."

"That's old?" Hickok glanced at Blade. "Are you dying off early because of advanced senility?"

"What do all of them words mean?"

"Old age?"

"Naw. No one lives to old age anymore. Most of us are killed by the time we're thirty."

"None of this makes any sense," Blade repeated. "I need to do some serious contemplating. We'll have a conference in the morning and consider our options."

"Don't strain your brain." Hickok grinned.

"Hey! Wait a minute!" Bertha said to Blade as he stood. "I've got a heap of questions of my own. Who's going to answer them?"

"I'll let Hickok handle the task." Blade smiled. "Joshua should be up here soon with your soup. You rest. We won't be leaving until you're fit to travel."

"Travel?"

"We need you to take us to the Twin Cities," Blade informed her.

"I don't know about that, honky." Bertha shook her head. "I'm finally free of that mess, and I'm not sure I want to go back. You can't know how bad it is there."

Blade walked to the doorway. "If you don't want to go, you don't have to. We won't force you to come with us. But it would make it easier on us if we had someone who knew their way around the Twin Cities."

"Why do you want to go there anyway?"

"H   ok can fill you in. I'm going to check our perimeter and insure the SEAL is secure. See you in the morning." Blade walked off.

"I like him," Bertha said to Hickok. "He's got a way about him."

"That he does," Hickok agreed.

Bertha rolled on her left side, facing Hickok. "I like you, too, White Meat."

"You certainly don't beat around the bush none, do you, girl?" Hickok admired her finely chiseled features.

"Life's too damn short to beat around the bush," she said sadly. "You gotta grab what you want, when you want it!"

"That's some philosophy."

"Tell me about yourself," she urged him. "I want to hear everything about you, and the others here with you, and where you come from, and what you're doing here, and why you want to go to the Twins."

"Anything else you want to know?" He grinned.

"You got a woman?" she bluntly demanded.

Hickok hesitated.

"Well, you got a woman or not? A simple yes or no will do just fine."

"No," Hickok said, his voice barely above a whisper. "I don't have a woman."

"Hmmmm." Bertha frowned. "I don't like the sound of that."

Joshua came into the room, carrying a steaming bowl of soup and a handful of jerky.

"Food!" Bertha struggled to sit up. Hickok assisted her. "I could eat a horse!"

"You're hungrier than when I left." Joshua placed the soup and jerky on the floor next to her legs. "I hope you enjoy this repast. I tried my best."

"Honey," she said, grabbing a stick of jerky, "this could be week-old dead skunk and I'd still gulp it down."

"I don't know if I could cook week-old dead skunk," Joshua said seriously.

Bertha smiled. "I like you too, beefcake! I like all of you."

"There's one of us you haven't met," Hickok told her.

"Oh? What's he like?"

"Ever heard of a book called *The Last of the Mohicans?*"

7

The Alpha Triad and Joshua met for a conference
early the next morning, sitting around the card
table. During the night the lights had flickered
several times, and finally the entire building had
plunged into darkness. Blade had made a torch
using a piece of cloth and a board, and they had
ventured downstairs. He had studied the generator
and found a cap on top of a tank, a cap similar to
one on the SEAL, and had recalled watching Plato
remove that cap and place an oil additive into the
engine. Blade had twisted the generator's cap off,
and had placed his nose over the hole. He could
smell a strong, acrid odor. A metal container had
rested on the floor. Acting on a hunch, Blade had
opened the container and discovered a liquid with
the same scent as the generator tank. Joshua had
held the torch to one side as Blade poured some of
the liquid into the tank. He had placed the cap
back in position and examined the front of the
generator. Three black buttons were situated to
the front. Arranged vertically, the top button was
labeled START, the center button STOP, and the
third something called CHOKE. Blade had pushed

the START button several times, and the generator had coughed and sputtered. He had stabbed the CHOKE button twice, had hit the START button, and had been delighted when the generator caught. The lights had come back on.

After breakfast, at the table, Geronimo complimented the Triad leader.

"That was a neat trick last night," he said. "Where'd you learn to start a generator?"

"Lucky guess," Blade replied. "I remembered Plato telling us about the fossil fuels the engines ran on before the Big Blast. When I saw the tank, and the container, I put two and two together."

Hickok yawned loudly. "Let's get this meeting over with. I need some more sleep."

"Poor baby," Geronimo ribbed him. "Serves you right for staying up most of the night."

"Bertha was asking more and more questions. Never saw such a curious woman. Wouldn't let me leave. I came down after she fell asleep. You sure she'll be all right?" He faced Joshua.

"She has suffered extensive surface damage," Joshua explained. "The beatings were severe. Fortunately, her vital organs were not injured. A few days rest, and plenty of nourishment, and she should be as good as new."

"Which brings us to this meeting." Blade got their attention. "We can use her. She knows the Twin Cities. She could make our job there a lot easier. Last night she told me she might not want to go back. Do we force her to against her will?"

"Definitely not," Joshua responded.

Geronimo shook his head.

"If the gal doesn't want to come with us, pard," Hickok said harshly, "she doesn't go with us."

"You're getting attached to her," Blade stated frankly.

"Bull!" Hickok said in denial. "She's a good kid.

She needs a friend, is all."

Blade suppressed a grin. "I didn't intend to force her to accompany us. I wanted to be sure how each of you felt. How long do you think we should stay in Thief River Falls? Until she is fully recovered? Until she's fit enough to travel, if she does elect to come with us?"

"I don't want to abandon her until she can take care of herself," Hickok said, expressing his opinion.

Blade tapped his finger on the table, pondering. "Agreed. We won't leave her until she's fit. I don't like the delay it's costing us, but we don't have any choice." His eyes ranged over each of them. "We do have a more serious problem to evaluate. Bertha told us about the Twin Cities last night. I couldn't understand everything, but enough to gether our trip there is going to be extremely dangerous. Several warring factions are fighting for control of the city, and we could find ourselves caught in the conflict. I'm not very optimistic about finding the equipment Plato needs either. Still, we've got to try."

"What about the Watchers?" Hickok asked. "We're bound to run into more of them."

"I know. We'll try to avoid them where possible. From what Bertha said, they're covering all the roads and highways out of the Twin Cities, exactly the same way they've covered the only highway heading south from the Home. Any ideas on who these Watchers are and where they come from?"

No one responded.

"I know." Blade shook his head. "We need more information. I did reach several conclusions concerning them. One, they have their base south of here."

"What makes you say that?" Geronimo asked.

"The Watcher named Joe made a reference to the

fact that Sammy, the one they take their orders from, is located south of here a ways, as he put it."

"He could easily have been lying," Geronimo pointed out.

"True," Blade admitted. "I don't doubt that much of what he told us was a smoke screen, but the statement concerning the location was ambiguous enough to be partially true." He paused. "My other conclusion is that the Watchers are containers."

"Come again?" Hickok's brow furrowed.

"Look at their pattern. Bertha says they surround the Twin Cities, preventing anyone from leaving. They also blocked the only major highway leading south from Home. Their policy seems to be one of containment, to prevent inhabited areas from spreading." Blade frowned. "One last item. Last night I remembered the leader of the Trolls saying they had a pact with the Watchers."

"What?" Hickok queried, startled, sitting up in his chair.

"I had no idea who he was talking about at the time," Blade explained. He looked at Joshua. "Any information you can supply?"

Joshua appeared taken off guard by the question. "What would I know?"

"You're one of the Family Empaths," Blade stated. "Plato has great confidence in your ability. Have you picked up anything, anything at all?"

Joshua lowered his eyes. "No."

"Keep trying," Blade ordered. "Do whatever it is you do, but get me something I can use."

"Get me a live Watcher," Joshua recommended.

"What?"

"My particular emphatic talent involves receiving impressions from objects and people, living people. I tried to imprint information from the bodies of the Watchers you killed, but I wasn't successful. Curious paradox. I can receive impressions from animate beings and inanimate objects, but not from inanimate beings. Interesting."

Hickok lazily stretched. "Any other items on our agenda this morning?"

"We've covered the essential points," Blade said. "We'll stay put until Bertha decides to come with us, if she does. Each of us will pull six-hour guard shifts, including you, Joshua. I realize you're not a Warrior, but everyone must participate."

"I understand," Joshua remarked.

"Hickok will provide you with one of the confiscated arms," Blade instructed.

"I will not bear arms," Joshua indignantly asserted.

"You will carry a gun on guard duty."

"It is against my personal philosophy to use a firearm." Joshua refused to budge.

"Using it is up to you," Blade countered. "But you will carry one, and that is final. If we're attacked, and you decide not to fire, at least shout a warning to alert us."

Joshua started to speak, then thought better of it.

"Geronimo," Blade went on, "you'll pull the first shift, so sleepyhead here," he nodded at Hickok, "can catch up on his beauty rest. The Spirit knows he needs it!"

"Thanks, pard," Hickok grumbled.

"When six hours are up, wake Hickok. Joshua, you're after Hickok. I'll pull the final shift. Any questions?"

"I have one," Hickok mentioned.

"Shoot."

Hickok grinned. "You keep mentioning six-hour shifts. How in the blazes are we supposed to know when six hours have gone by? We left our hour-glasses back at the Home, and the sundial was just too plain big to tote along.''

Blade removed an item from his right front pocket. "I think this will suffice."

"I don't believe it!" Hickok gaped.

"Where'd you get that? I didn't see it when I stripped the bodies," Geronimo said.

"Is that a watch?" Joshua asked.

Blade nodded. "That's what they were called. It was on the guy called Joe. I removed it before you searched their clothes," he answered Geronimo. "It's making a sound, like a scratching, and the black pointers are moving, so I assume it's still working."

"May I?" Joshua reached over and took the watch. "I remember reading something about these things in the library. These pointers were called hands, I believe. If I recall correctly, this watch is indicating it's seven in the morning."

"Thank the Founder for the library," Geronimo stated.

Blade mentally agreed. Kurt Carpenter had stocked almost five hundred thousand books in E Block, shelf after shelf of the greatest literature mankind had produced, the classics, interspersed with sections devoted to specific topics or themes. One of the largest sections was exclusively devoted to survival skills. Reference books on every conceivable subject were at the Family's fingertips. Books on military tactics and strategies. Gardening. Hunting and fishing. Woodworking. Metalsmithing. Natural medicine. Weaving and sewing. History books. Geography books. Volumes on religion and philosophy. Dictionaries. Encyclopedias. Fiction for entertainment. Humorous books, like the Peanuts and Garfield cartoon collections. And on and on. Carpenter had tried to envision the challenges the Family would face, and to stock books instructing the Family on how to cope with those obstacles. How-to books were present in abundance. Carpenter never realized it, but his library would become the Family's prime source of amusement as well as tutelage. With the demise of electricity, most contemporary diversions faded into oblivion. Not so with the books. Family children were taught to read at an early age, and reading became a primarly Family pursuit. Everyone read. Most read avidly. Photographic books were especially prized, many of the photos of prewar culture and technology evoking awe and wonder. Reading and music were the Family's recreation. Plato had once mentioned to Blade that he preferred it that way. Blade had inquired as to why. "These pastimes sharpen the intellect. Most of those before the war atrophied the brain," Plato had said.

"How do you tell what time it is?" Hickok leaned toward Joshua.

Joshua held the watch so Hickok could see. "The big pointer, or hand, tells you the minute. The smaller hand tells you the hour."

"What's that third hand do?" Hickok asked. "The thin one."

Joshua reflected a moment. "I think that tells you about the seconds."

Hickok sadly shook his head. "I never would have made it," he dryly commented.

"Made what?" Joshua inquired.

"Made it before the Big Blast. First the SEAL. Now this watch. Everything back then was so blasted complicated!"

"All it takes is practice," Geronimo said, disagreeing. "You'll change your mind once you get the hang of things."

"Bet me," Hickok quipped.

"Here." Joshua gave the watch to Geronimo.

"You have the first shift and you'll need this."

Geronimo studied the time. "So if I understand you, I wake up Hickok at one to pull his shift."

"You got it," Blade told him and pushed back from the table. "I think I'm going to search some of the other buildings, see what I can find."

"Probably nothing," Hickok predicted. "There's just us and the dead Watchers and that's it, folks."

The scream, a terrified, penetrating shriek, punctuated Hickok's statement.

"That came from upstairs!" Joshua shouted.

Hickok was already in motion, scooping up his Henry from where he had placed it against his chair and bounding up the steps.

Blade, Geronimo, and Joshua quickly followed.

The petrified cry was just fading when the four men piled into Bertha's room.

"What is it?" Hickok asked, glancing at the window, which was still closed.

Bertha was sitting up, the blanket clutched in front of her body, covering her to the chin. She was staring, wide-eyed, at an opening at the base of the room's south wall, a former vent, the cover since removed by a previous tenant.

"Kill it!" she beseeched them, her voice shrill. "Kill the damn thing!"

Perched on its rear legs in the vent opening stood a large rat, its whiskers twitching, defiantly gazing at them.

"It's just a rat," Hickok said, amazed. He stared down at Bertha. "You're afraid of one measly old rat?"

"Kill it!" She frantically clutched his left leg. "For God's sake, kill it before it can bring the rest back here!"

"Whatever you say." Hickok began to bring the Henry up, but stopped when Blade grabbed his arm.

"Not in here," Blade nodded at the rifle. "Think of our ears." He was holding his Commando in his left hand, his right slowly sneaking around his back, to the Solingen thowing knifes.

"Oh, get it, please!" Bertha whispered.

The rat dropped to all fours and began to turn, to leave.

Blade crouched, sweeping his right hand forward, gripping the Solingen by the tip of the blade. He threw overhand, the knife turning end over end as it crossed the six feet between them and imbedded itself to the hilt in the rat's fat, squat body.

The rat reared back, screeching and chittering, clawing at the knife. The furry body was racked with intense spasms. It squealed one final time, tottered on the edge of the vent, and toppled over, disappearing down the shaft.

"My knife!" Blade lunged for the opening, too late. His fingers clutched empty air. "Damn!" He knelt and peered down the vent. "Can't see a thing! I'll never get that knife back."

Bertha sank to the mattress, trembling.

Hickok dropped to his knees and cradled her in his arms. "Come on, Black Beauty. It's dead and gone. You can relax."

Bertha struggled to sit up, glaring at each of them. "Don't you fools understand?"

"Understand what?" Hickok answered her.

"About rats."

"What's the big deal over one rat? We see them from time to time around our Home, but they're no problem."

"This ain't your Home, White Meat," she reminded him. "In the cities it's different. I didn't think they would be in a small town like this, but I guess I was wrong. You should see them in the Twins!" She shuddered. "Millions and millions of them. Mostly they keep to themselves in the sewers and underground tunnels, but they come up from time to time, roaming the streets, hunting.''

Blade recalled an earlier statement she had made. "Do the rats eat the Wacks you were telling us about? You said the Wacks use the underground too."

Bertha was staring at the vent. "They eat each other, far as I know," she replied absently. "The Wacks got fire, though, and the rats don't like fire none. They're terrible, but they can't hold a candle to the roaches."

"The roaches?" It was Joshua's turn to ask, perplexed.

"The cockroaches," Bertha responded. "More cockroaches than a person could count."

"Don't tell me the bugs are dangerous?" Hickok cracked.

Bertha gazed at Hickok. "I pity you, White Meat. You got so much to learn. You can stomp a Wack easy enough, if they don't nail you first. Even the rats can be stabbed or shot or clubbed for as long as you got your strength. But the cockroaches! How you gonna fight a horde of bugs only six inches long and two inches wide?"

"How big?" Blade interjected, doubting he'd heard her correctly. Out of the corner of his eye he saw Geronimo leave the room.

Bertha raised her hands and held them the proper distance apart. "This long."

Hickok whistled. "How the blazes do you stand living in the Twin Cities?"

"I can't stand it," she answered, "which is why I want out. I don't never want to go back there. No way."

"Whatever you decide," Blade told her. "Just keep in mind we could really use your help. We need a guide, someone who knows their way around the Twin Cities. Someone who could help us find the things we're looking for."

Bertha shook her head. "No way, man. I'd have to be stone cold crazy to go back there."

"Won't Z be expecting you back?" Hickok asked her.

"Hey, White Meat," she said, shrugging, "it's a dog-eat-dog world. Z won't miss me. If I hadn't got myself caught by the Watchers, maybe I would have gone back and reported it. But I did get nabbed, and I had a lot of time to think while they was beating me and burning me and poking me, and I made a decision. Bertha, I told myself, if, by some miracle, you get out of this mess, then there ain't no way, no how, you're going back to the Twins. I tell you, I'd be crazy to go back there!"

Blade could see the subject distressed her. "Whatever you say," he stated. "You get your rest. We've decided to stay with you until you can take care of yourself. Then we'll be leaving for the Twin Cities."

"Can't you leave it alone?" she pleaded. "Can't you just go back to this Home you're from and forget the Twins?"

Blade shook his head. "No. A lot of people, people we love dearly, are relying on us. We must get to the Twins."

"White Meat told me you got a woman waiting for you," Bertha said, trying another tack. "Don't you want to see her again?"

"Of course I do," Blade replied, an edge to his voice.

"Well, you won't if you go on the way you are," Bertha ventured. "None of you will come back from the Twins."

"We'll take that chance." Blade spun and left the room. He hurried downstairs, his anger building. How dare she remind him of Jenny! He walked outside.

Geronimo was holding his Browning, leaning against the front of the SEAL. He noticed Blade's expression.

"You okay?" Geronimo solicitously inquired.

"Fine," Blade replied, too quickly, the word a growl in his deep chest.

Geronimo turned away, knowing his friend all too well. Blade was known for a long fuse, but when he blew, watch out! His temper was renowned in the Family. Geronimo grinned, remembering the time Blade took on an entire pack of wild dogs with just his Bowies in his hands, his face flushed with pure rage, determined to hack the canines to pieces! A firm hand fell on his left shoulder, and he turned.

"Sorry," Blade said simply.

"No problem."

Blade smiled and strolled off. He headed west, skirting the park, thinking of Jenny. Was she up already? Was she still pining for him? Would she cry herself to sleep at night until he returned? Dear Spirit, how he missed her! He wanted to get this damn trip over with as fast as humanly possible and return to the Home!

The bright sun on his face brought him up short. He gazed upward, watching several white clouds drifting eastward. The sky was tinged with a shade of gray today, as it sometimes was. Periodically, the entire sky would turn a somber shade of cement gray, the air filled with tiny particles of ash and dust.

Blade's mind drifted, recollecting the Family records concerning the aftermath of the Third World War. Carpenter had been delightfully surprised the fallout at the Home was minimal. He had expected to see higher concentrations, particularly if the missile silos in North Dakota were hit with ground blasts of ten megatons or more. Fortunately for the fate of the Home, at the time of the Soviet attack on the North Dakota missile fields, the prevailing winds at the forty-thousand-foot altitude, the air currents responsible for the primary distribution of the fallout, had been bearing in a southeasterly direction, not toward the east. So the Family had escaped the brunt of the fallout. It could not, however, avoid other inevitable consequences of a nuclear war.

The thousands of nuclear explosions had forced huge amounts of dust and ash into the atmosphere. Volcanic activity had abruptly increased, becoming widespread. A dark cloud had choked the sky for over five years, eventually dispersing. Now, a century later, the conditions were nearly similar to before the Big Blast, except for periodic clouds of volcanic residue.

Another repercussion of the thermonuclear conflict was the reduction of the ozone layer. The nitrogen oxides created by the mushroom clouds ate at the ozone, causing solar ultraviolet levels to rise tremendously. For a decade after the war, anyone who ventured outdoors without adequate protective clothing had suffered a prompt, blistering sunburn. Certain plant strains had been completely eliminated.

All of these memories filtered through Blade's mind as he gazed up at the sky.

A rustling of tree leaves drew his attention to his right. He twisted, studying the tree, an oak with wide, sweeping branches. The rustling had stopped.

Blade looked over his shoulder. He was out of sight of the concrete building, standing near the park. The undergrowth was dense and prolific. His senses suddenly shrieked a warning, trying to alert him that something was amiss.

But what?

Blade gripped the Commando in both hands and approached the edge of the park.

Was it a mutate?

Blade crouched near a clump of tall grass, scanning the shadows, prepared.

He thought.

A huge, gnarled, brown hand unexpectedly parted the grass, exposing a face filled with malevolent intent.

Blade caught a brief glimpse of two large brown eyes, of a large, crooked nose, almost beaklike, of a gaping mouth filled with pointed teeth, and his nose was overwhelmed by an obnoxious stench, just as the thing pounced.

Blade's attacker was a gigantic, lumbering brute. It slammed into Blade, sending him sprawling, the Commando flying to one side. The thing bellowed and jumped, aiming both heels at Blade's head.

Blade instinctively rolled, avoiding the crushing blow. He automatically noted his assailant was only wearing a buckskin loincloth, that its thick body was burned black and pitted and scarred over every inch.

The thing roared and leaped, catching Blade around the neck in an iron grip. Its fingers closed in an inexorable vise.

Blade felt his body being lifted off the ground, his feet dangling and helpless. He tried to focus, to gather his wits. Concentrating, he brought his hands up, smashing them against the thing's ears.

The brute ignored the blow.

Blade swung his arms again, his thumbs extended, plunging them into the short, squat neck.

The brute gurgled, but the choking hold did not slacken.

Blade tried another move, feeling his chest
beginning to ache, his wind cut off, his lungs
craving air. He held his hands in the Crane style of
offense and stabbed them directly into the leering
brown eyes.

The giant roared and released Blade, covering its
eyes.

Blade drew his right Bowie, his motion practiced
and fluid as he imbedded the blade in the brute's
chest to the hilt.

The thing uncovered its eyes and gaped at the
knife sticking in its chest. It looked up at Blade.
And grinned.

Blade, astonished, didn't see the blow that sent
him reeling to the ground. He felt blood filling his
mouth and he rose to his knees, trying to regain his
footing before it attacked him again.

Too late.

The brute clamped the neck choke on him again,
twisting its fingers, this time attempting to snap
the spinal column.

Blade's vision spun.

Think, damn you, he told himself. Think! The
worst reaction right now would be mindless panic.
He couldn't rise, the thing was holding him down.
Even his strength was as nothing compared to this
giant. He gripped his left Bowie. Out of the corner
of his left eye he could see one huge, naked foot. It
was the only possible target. He swung the knife
backward and down, and he knew he had connected, knew the blade had sliced through the
foot and stuck in the ground.

The brute shrieked and released Blade. It hopped
up and down on one foot, trying to grab the Bowie
and pull it free.

Blade sagged to the ground, wheezing, gasping
for air. He tried to reach for the dagger on his right
leg, but his fingers abruptly went weak, drooping.

Dear Spirit, no! He had to defend himself or he was as good as dead!

The thing had managed to grip the handle of the Bowie and yank. Blood spurted as the blade pulled loose. The brute held the knife up and appeared to study it for a moment, then it tossed the Bowie aside. Growling, it pulled the other Bowie from its immense chest and flung the knife to the ground.

Blade took hold of the dagger and braced himself. If the Bowie knives couldn't affect this giant, what good would a dagger do?

The brute bent down, its long, hairy arms reaching for its intended victim.

Blade rammed his dagger into the creature's throat and twisted, gratified when blood gushed over his arm.

The thing gurgled and gasped, pulling away from Blade.

Now was his chance!

Blade leaped to his feet, scooping up one of his Bowies. He swung the big knife, slicing the brute's midriff.

The creature had pressed its hands against its neck, striving to stem the flow of crimson. It roared as the Bowie bit into its stomach again and attempted to grab its assailant.

Blade dropped and stepped back, trying to pinpoint the brute's must vulnerable point. He heard footsteps behind him.

"I heard all the commotion," Geronimo announced. "Let me finish this thing for you."

"Be my guest."

The monstrosity came at them as Geronimo fired, voicing his war whoop. The shot struck the thing in the chest, blowing the flesh apart. Incredibly, the giant staggered, but recovered and took two steps forward. The Browning roared twice more, the ruptured chest spattering blood and flesh everywhere. This time, the brute went down, toppling like a felled tree.

"Are you seriously injured?" Geronimo asked Blade, concern carved on his face.

"I don't think so," Blade replied, breathing deeply.

"You look a mess."

"Thanks."

Geronimo walked over to the thing, staring in amazement. "What is this? It's not a mutate. I've never seen anything like it."

"Beats me." Blade shrugged. He retrieved his weapons.

"Think there could be more of them?" Geronimo nervously asked.

Blade stopped, searching the nearby trees and grass. "Could be. I say we get back to the others."

"Looks like they had the idea first." Geronimo grinned, pointing.

Hickok and Joshua were running toward them, Hickok with his Pythons in his hands, Joshua holding a shotgun.

"What the hell is going on?" Hickok demanded as they ran up.

Blade nodded at the brute.

"What the blazes . . .?" Hickok began, fascinated by the hulk lying on the ground.

"Not another one!" Joshua exclaimed. He stood behind Hickok, and his view was obstructed.

"Not human anyway." Hickok stepped to one side so Joshua could see clearly.

"What is it?" Joshua wanted to know.

"You tell us," Geronimo countered.

They silently studied the creature, a dozen questions filling their minds.

"What do we do with it?" Joshua eventually inquired.

"Nothing," Blade answered. His neck was

throbbing and a headache was starting to form.

"We don't bury it?" Joshua gasped at the shredded chest.

Hickok looked at Joshua and frowned. "Be serious."

"I should know better by now," Joshua admitted.

"Where's your Henry?" Geronimo asked Hickok.

"Left it with Bertha when we heard the shots. She was still antsy over the rat deal. Thought she'd feel safer if she had the Henry."

"Where'd you get that?" Blade inquired of Joshua, indicating the pump shotgun.

"Hickok gave it to me," Joshua said sheepishly.

"I took it from the guy Geronimo shot yesterday," Hickok informed Blade, "the one we first saw on the roof. It's a Smith and Wesson Model 3000 Pump. You told him to get a gun. He doesn't have any firing experience, and if he should decide to let loose . . ."

"I will not kill a brother or sister," Joshua interrupted.

" . . . even if it's just to warn us," Hickok continued as if Joshua hadn't spoken, "then the shotgun should suffice. A lot of firepower, but you don't need to be able to hit a knothole at fifty yards to be effective with it."

"Any ammo for it?" Blade asked.

Hickok nodded. "Yep. Found a dozen spare rounds, all slugs, in the Watcher's pockets. Probably more in that storage room we found upstairs."

"Good." Blade surveyed the nearby foliage. "We'll head back. If there is another one of these things lurking about," he kicked the dead brute, "we'll fare better if we stay in groups. So from now on, we only go outside in pairs. No one goes outdoors alone. Is that clearly understood?"

"You bet, pard," Hickok replied.

"Absolutely," Geronimo answered.

Joshua nodded his understanding.

"Okay. Let's head back. Keep on your toes."

They cautiously returned to their temporary headquarters. Blade took the point, alert for any unusual sounds or movements. His neck was beginning to swell and his throat felt dry. Some water would taste wonderful! He speculated on his attacker. What had the thing been? It appeared to be more human than animal, but it acted bestial in every other respect. Where did it come from? Was it an isolated freak of nature, or just one of a species? Why hadn't they ever seen one near the Home? Thank the Spirit they hadn't! The mutates were bad enough, without having to worry about this new threat.

They rounded a turn and saw the SEAL ahead.

"Everything looks all right," Hickok commented.

The muted blast of the Henry, three times, galvanized them into immediate action.

"Bertha!" Hickok exclaimed, running for the concrete building.

"Geronimo," Blade ordered as he ran, following on Hickok's heels, "stay outside with Joshua! Watch the SEAL!"

Blade followed Hickok into the building and up the stairs. As they reached the second floor the Henry boomed again.

"Take that, sucker!" they heard Bertha yell as they burst into her room.

Four dead rats were clustered around the vent opening in the wall.

"Got 'em." Bertha beamed at Hickok and Blade. "They thought they was gonna make a meal of me, but I showed them!"

Blade walked to the vent and knelt, listening. From the dark depths below came scratching sounds. "There's more down there."

"Of course," Bertha said. "Rats travel in packs. Just 'cause we've killed some of 'em won't stop 'em. They'll be back for their supper."

"I don't understand," Hickok stated. "Why are they attacking us? Did they bother you once the whole time you were in this room before we arrived?"

Bertha thought a second. "Nope. Sure didn't."

"Then why are they suddenly concentrating here?" Hickok asked.

"Beats me, White Meat."

Blade stood. "Bertha, what attracts rats?"

"Food mostly. Any kind of food. They'll eat practically anything. Grain. Fruit. Meat. They like garbage. Dead bodies are real popular too."

"Dead bodies?" Blade repeated, jarred by an idea.

"Yeah. Dead bodies will attract them rats like nothing else will. Bring 'em in from miles and miles around."

"Dead bodies," Blade said again, comprehension dawning.

Blade faced Bertha. "Didn't you say the rats live underground?"

"Yeah. In the sewers and other tunnels."

Blade glanced at Hickok. "And where did Geronimo tell us he dropped the dead Watchers?"

"I know!" Hickok exclaimed. "Down some opening in the middle of the street!"

"What? You dropped those bodies down to the rats? You fed the rats?" Bertha asked, astonished.

"We weren't aware the rats were down there," Blade explained.

"How could anyone be so stupid?" Bertha made a clicking sound. "Honkies never stop amazing me."

"So the bodies drew in all the rats under Thief River Falls," Blade reasoned. "Rats that would normally be scattered in miles and miles of tunnels are converging on this area, drawn by the dead Watchers."

"Who have probably been eaten by now," Bertha mentioned.

"So the rats are spreading out, searching for other food in this immediate area, searching for . . ." Blade paused.

"For us!" Bertha finished for him.

"Damn!" Hickok glared at the dead rats.

"How many rats can there be?" Blade asked.

"Beats me, sugar." Bertha shrugged. "Like I told you, under the Twins there's millions and millions of 'em. Under a town this size, who knows? Probably thousands."

"What do we do?" Hickok interjected. "Leave?"

"Not until we've taken the generator and the other supplies and hidden them somewhere safe from the Watchers and the rats," Blade stated.

"I hope you've got a plan, pard," Hickok said anxiously. "Being eaten by a rat isn't my idea of going out in style."

"I have a plan," Blade assured him.

"Then let's get to it."

Blade stared at Bertha. "Think you're up to being moved?"

Bertha surprised both of them by rising swiftly to her feet. "I can move myself, thank you. I'm feeling lots stronger."

"Don't push yourself," Blade warned. "Just take your blanket downstairs. We'll bring the mattress down in a bit."

"Okay by me."

Blade's plan took an hour to complete. They lugged the mattress downstairs and placed it along the bar. Despite her protests, they insisted Bertha lie down and rest. Blade left Geronimo in the doorway on guard, and directed Joshua and Hickok to carry all of the supplies in the one upstairs room down to the first floor. The supplies would be stacked near the door until they decided where they intended to hide their windfall. Blade, meanwhile, found several loose boards behind the bar. He took two and went back to Bertha's former room. Using three bottles of whiskey, he propped one of the boards over the vent opening. Blade wished he had a hammer and nails, but they hadn't brought any from the Home and he didn't know if the Watchers kept any tools. The board would effectively block any light from seeping down the vent, and he suspected the light attracted the rats to potential openings. On tiptoe, he reached up and removed the lightbulb in the overhead light, plunging the room into darkness. He exited, closing the door behind him. There was a thin crack between the bottom of the door and the floor. He pressed the other board against the opening to further prevent light from seeping in.

Next Blade checked the vents in the other two upstairs rooms. Unlike the open vent in Bertha's room, the other vents were covered with a sturdy metal grill. Blade doubted the rats could gain access using them.

That left the basement.

Blade passed Hickok and Joshua in the hallway. "How's it coming?"

"Four or five more trips should do it," Hickok replied.

"I'll help you if I get done first," Blade offered.

"Fine." Hickok stopped at the storeroom doorway. "Say, pard, what the blazes is a peach?"

"A what?" Blade paused at the head of the stairs.

"A peach. Found a box of cans labeled fruit. Some cans of apples and others of pears. Six cans of peaches, whatever they are. Ever heard of them?"

"No."

"I believe I saw pictures of them in one of the books," Joshua mentioned.

"Can we have some for the noon meal?" Hickok asked Blade.

"Don't see why not." Blade smiled and headed for the basement.

The basement door was in a far corner at the end of the bar.

"Hey, Blade," Bertha spoke up as Blade passed her. "Was them bottles of whiskey I saw?"

"That's what the Watcher called it," Blade told her.

"How's about getting me one when you have time?"

"You got it."

Blade reached the basement door and slowly opened it. There was one dim light in the basement, placed in a dirty socket in the center of the ceiling. The generator was aligned along the north wall.

Would there be rats down there?

Blade raised his Commando and inched forward, taking the stairs one hesitant step at a time. If the rats could gain entry to the basement, they might swarm him before he had a chance to fire. Where were the vents?

A squeaking sound came from his right.

Blade pivoted, searching.

Nothing but a brick wall. The sound, apparently, came from behind the wall.

More squeaking and rustling, from all walls.

The rats had the basement surrounded!

Blade stopped. Did the underground tunnels pass by the basement? Were the rodents attempting to dig their way in or merely passing by the wall on the other side? He didn't hear any digging noises.

The generator was running smoothly, emitting a mild rumbling sound. He spotted an open metal box, full of tools, under the tank.

Was that it? Would the rats shy away from something as alien as the generator? Could they hear or feel the vibrations?

Blade checked the entire basement.

No vents!

Blade smiled, relieved. The rats would need to dig their way in. Before going upstairs, he opened the cap on the generator tank and checked the fluid level. The tank was still three-fourths full. Good.

"Hey, Blade!" Bertha yelled down the stairs.

Quickly, Blade replaced the cap and ran up the steps, closing the door behind him.

Bertha was sitting on her mattress, holding the Henry in her lap. "Geronimo wants you," she said as Blade emerged from the basement.

Blade joined Geronimo by the doorway.

"Saw something," Geronimo stated. He was staring at the park on the other side of the street.

"What was it?" Blade scanned the vegetation.

"Don't know. A glimpse of something big and brown. Do you want me to investigate?"

Blade thoughtfully chewed his lower lip. "No. Might be another one like the thing that attacked me."

"What if it steps into the open?"

"Kill it," Blade directed.

Geronimo nodded.

Blade walked to the table and sat down. Big brown brutes outside, hordes of rats inside. More Watchers might return at any time. Blade frowned. He had wanted to stay put until Bertha was recovered from her ordeal, until she was fit enough to travel without hardship. That option was becoming untenable. Too many threats faced them if they remained in Thief River Falls. The mission came first. Getting to the Twin Cities was their paramount concern, eclipsing all other considerations. Besides, the faster this trip went, the sooner they'd see the Home again.

Hickok and Joshua were walking by the table, their arms laden with supplies.

"I thought you said you'd give us a hand," Hickok reminded him.

"Have something to attend to first," Blade replied. He stood and walked behind the bar. The whiskey bottles were standing under the counter on a shelf located on the left side of the bar. He grabbed one of the bottles by the neck.

"What have you got there?" Bertha asked him as he came around the bar and sat down on the floor next to her mattress.

"Isn't this what you wanted?" He displayed the bottle.

"Lordy!" Her eyes widened. "Prime drinkin' whiskey! Can't hardly believe it! That stuff sure is hard to come by in the Twins." She reached for the bottle.

Blade hesitated. "You sure this stuff is good for you in your condition?"

"I ain't having a baby, honey." She impatiently took the bottle.

"Would you like something to eat?" Blade inquired.

"I never drink on a full stomach." She grinned, looking at him expectantly, then frowning when he didn't laugh. "Don't you get it? I never drink on a full stomach."

"I distinctly heard your statement," Blade responded. "Why? Does it have some special significance?"

"Ain't you ever drank whiskey before?" Bertha unscrewed a black plastic cap.

"No."

"No?" She gawked, unbelieving.

"No. Why?"

Bertha laughed. "Here. I'll let you go first. Take a deep swig."

Blade held the bottle in his right hand. "A deep swig?"

"The deeper, the better." Bertha grinned. "This stuff will set your hair on fire."

"Why would I want to set my hair on fire?"

"Just drink the damn whiskey," she urged him.

Blade shrugged, tipped the bottle, and swallowed as much as he possibly could in one gulp.

"That's it!"

Blade placed the bottle on the floor, wondering what in the world she was grinning about, considering her a bit strange, when the whiskey hit him. A tremendous burning sensation exploded in his stomach, his throat tingling, his mouth puckering. He screwed up his face and glared at the bottle.

Bertha was laughing hysterically, slapping her hands on her thighs. "Oh, beautiful! Just beautiful!"

Blade began coughing uncontrollably, his eyes watering.

"Blade, you're something else!"

Hickok and Joshua walked over.

"What the blazes is going on here?" Hickok demanded.

"I'm making a man out of your friend here," Bertha was still giggling.

"You're what?"

Bertha picked up the whiskey bottle. "Here. Try this. You'll see what I mean."

Hickok raised the bottle to his nose and sniffed.

"Thanks, but no thanks." He gave the bottle to Bertha.

"What's wrong?" she asked, surprised.

"That stuff smells awful," Hickok said. "I have this policy against drinking anything that smells like horse piss."

Bertha shook her head. "You boys sure are weird! Any man in the Twins would kill for a drink of this."

"We're not from the Twins," Hickok stated.

"That, White Meat, is what makes you so beautiful." She beamed up at him.

Blade had stopped sputtering and wheezing.

"What'd you think?" Bertha smiled.

"Terrible!" Blade exclaimed, his voice a ragged whisper. "But I think it killed the pain in my throat."

Bertha gulped several mouthfuls. "This stuff will sure enough kill whatever ails you," she agreed.

"Are you finished with the supplies?" Blade faced Hickok.

"Almost."

"Would you get it done as quickly as you can? I need to talk with Bertha. Alone," he emphasized.

Hickok stared from one to the other. "Whatever you say, pard." He strolled off, Joshua in tow.

Bertha swigged some more whiskey. "What do you want to talk with me about?"

"The Twins."

Bertha frowned. "I told you last night, Blade. I ain't goin' back there. Not for any reason."

"What if I can give you a good reason?"

"Fat chance."

"How would you like to come live with us at our home?"

Bertha paused, the bottle touching her lips. "Say what?"

Blade smiled. "I asked if you would like to live with us?"

"Are you serious?"

"Completely."

"You mean I could?" She set the bottle on the floor.

"Would you like to?"

"White Meat told me all about this Home of yours," Bertha said softly. "Sounds too good to be true. You just can't imagine how bad it is in the Twins. The Home almost sounds like heaven."

"Then you'd like to come back there with us?"

"What's the catch?" she eyed him warily.

"Catch?"

"Don't play innocent with me! White Meat also told me that you're one clever son of a bitch. What's your angle?"

Blade stared gravely into her eyes. "Be our guide when we reach Twin Cities, help us, and we'll take you back to the Home when we return."

"You mean if you return," she said, disgusted. "I knew it! I knew there'd be a catch!"

Blade remained silent.

"Tell me, Blade." She grinned craftily. "What's to stop me from going to the Home on my own? From what I've learned, the folks there are real nice. Nicer than you anyway. I bet they'd take me right in, no questions asked."

"They probably would," Blade agreed. "The question, though, is whether you could find the Home on your own. Do you think you could without a map? And remember, the country around the Home is literally swarming with mutates. How do you expect to get by them? It'd be awful rough going for one person."

"I could do it," Bertha said, her tone lacking conviction.

"Then forget I brought the subject up." Blade

made a move to rise.

"Wait!" she said hastily. "Don't be in such a hurry. I'm thinking it over."

"Listen, Bertha." Blade held her eyes with his own. "I'm not trying to pressure you . . ."

"Don't jive me, honky!"

". . . because in the final analysis the decision is all yours. You don't have to come with us to the Twins. Stay here in Thief River Falls and we'll pick you up on our way back to the Home."

"If you make it back!" she snorted.

"My point exactly. Which is why we need you. We have a better chance of making it with you to aid us. You can still stay here if you like. We'll leave you ample food and ammunition. But what happens if the Watchers pay this place a visit? They must make periodic supply runs from wherever their headquarters is located. What about the rats? Do you really want to stay here alone?"

Bertha glanced around the room, her brow knit in thought. "Nope," she answered at last. "I guess I don't."

"You really don't have that many options," Blade stressed. "I appreciate how you feel about the Twins, and I know you detest the thought of going back, but it really is your safest bet."

"Maybe White Meat would stay here with me until you get back." She grasped at one last straw.

"Hickok is a Warrior. He would never desert his Triad."

"You think so?"

"Do you want to ask him?"

Hickok and Joshua were descending the stairs with yet another load of provisions.

Bertha gazed at the gunman. "No. Don't bother him. I'd hate to put the burden on him."

"Then you'll come with us to the Twin Cities?"

"What choice have I got?" she said quietly, sadly.

Blade reached out and squeezed her right shoulder. "Don't worry. We'll take real good care of you."

"There's just one thing that bothers me about that."

"What?"

"Who the hell is going to take care of you?"

8

Blade called a meeting and informed the rest of Bertha's decision to accompany them. He explained his motives for leaving Thief River Falls before the day was out.

"First, we can't be positive the Watchers won't return in sufficient force to give us real trouble. Secondly, the rats might decide we're too tempting a meal to pass up and attack us en masse. Third, there's a possibility that whatever jumped me earlier has friends waiting outside to ambush us after dark. Finally, we're under a time constraint to return to our Family. I've decided we leave before sundown."

Blade, Hickok, and Joshua were sitting at the table. Bertha was lying on her mattress. Geronimo stood at the door.

"What about Bertha?" Hickok protested. "Is she fit enough to travel?"

"Don't worry about me none, White Meat," Bertha chimed in. "I'll manage."

"We'll clear a space in the rear of the SEAL for her," Blade detailed. "She'll be comfortable and safer than she would be in here."

"What about all of this?" Geronimo pointed at the stack of boxes.

"We load all of that into the SEAL, along with the generator, and transport it to a building on the western edge of town. Put it on the second floor in a room we can seal and protect from the rats. If the Watchers return and find it missing, I doubt they'd take the time to search every abandoned building in Thief River Falls. It would take them weeks." Blade gazed at each of them. "Any questions? Disagreements? Now's the time to let me know."

"I would enjoy moving on," Joshua said. "This place fills me with vivid memories of violent death."

"I like it," Geronimo concurred.

"I reckon it's okay by me, pard." Hickok was staring at Bertha.

"Good. Joshua, Geronimo, and I will load the SEAL and hide the provisions. Hickok, you stay here and guard Bertha." Blade stood.

"Thanks, Blade." Hickok smiled at his friend and walked over to Bertha. "Looks like you got me babysitting you for a spell, Black Beauty."

"Will you burp me too?"

Hickok grinned. "I'll paddle you if you don't behave yourself."

"Yes, mother."

"Get some rest."

Bertha closed her eyes. "Funny," she said in a whisper. "This is the first time in years I'm going to sleep feelin' safe and protected."

"Before you doze off," Hickok mentioned, "would you answer a question?"

"What?"

"Why're you doing this? Going to the Twin Cities? I thought you'd never go back there."

Bertha stared at the ceiling. "I just changed my mind, is all."

"Why?" he pressured her.

"Your friend made me see the light."

"Blade? What'd he say?"

"Not much."

"Come on!"

"Really."

Hickok watched Blade heft a box and carry it outside to the SEAL. "He's my best friend, Bertha. If he said something I'm going to regret, I need to know."

"He just told it like it is."

"All right," Hickok said gruffly. "Drop the subject."

Bertha touched his arm. "Besides, Hickok, you know by now I kind of got a thing for you. You're the prettiest honky I've ever seen."

Hickok opened his mouth to speak, but changed his mind.

"I don't want to let you out of my sight." Bertha grinned. "Another woman might come along and steal you away."

Hickok, uncomfortable, twisted and stared off into the distance. Blast her! Why did she flaunt her affection? Couldn't she just let events develop naturally? He smiled. The girl sure had a heap of spunk! What was her background like? he wondered. Her description of life in the Twin Cities was terrible! It was amazing she still retained a sense of humor after what she had been through. He thought of the Watchers, grimacing. For what they had done to her, for the indignities and the humiliation and the pain, they would pay! He would see to it personally. Every Watcher he met from this day on would be a dead Watcher shortly after their meeting. Joshua, in a sense, was correct. No one had the right to inflict such abuse on another human being. They would be made to pay. Hickok recalled a portion of the Bible he'd read, something about an eye for an eye. That was his idea of justice. Swift, effective, and personal.

Hickok thought of Joshua. Had Joshua learned anything from the experience of the past two days? Didn't he know by now that the men and women of the world were drastically different from the Family, that they didn't cherish the same spiritual and moral values? Hickok felt pity for Joshua. In the confines of the Home, protected by the walls and the Warriors, insulated from the outside world, Joshua could pursue peaceful pastimes, ignoring the grim realities of existence, living love and promoting truth. Now, exposed and vulnerable, Joshua was finding it difficult to cope, to adjust to a system of survival based on a primal urge: kill or be killed. Without the Warriors along, Joshua would have died two days ago. Why had Plato sent him along? What sort of balance could Joshua provide if he bawled his brains out every time they shot an enemy? It didn't make much sense to him, but then those highbrows never did. All that thinking warped the brain. Give him a decent, stand-up shootout any old day. His basic instincts had served him in good stead all these years, and if he continued to trust them, to act on them, his chances of surviving were better than Joshua's would ever be.

Memories of Joan filled his mind, unbidden, disturbing, filling him with feelings of guilt and betrayal. After all, it was only a month or so ago she was killed by the Trolls, and here he was experiencing an attraction toward Bertha, a woman he hardly knew. Was his budding affection for Bertha genuine, or was she catching him on the rebound? Was it Bertha's personality he liked, or her strength, her toughness, so very reminiscent of Joan?

The sound of the SEAL's engine turning over shattered his reverie.

Hickok glanced up.

Geronimo was standing in the doorway. All of the confiscated supplies had been loaded on the SEAL.

"We're taking off to hide the boxes," Geronimo said. "We shouldn't be too long. Watch yourself."

"Piece of cake."

Geronimo smiled, waved, and ran to the SEAL.

Hickok walked to the door and watched the transport drive off, Blade behind the wheel. They'd need to return for the generator.

Outside, in the bright sunlight, the park appeared tranquil and picturesque.

So what should he do while they were gone?

Hickok gazed at Bertha. She was sleeping, her breathing deep and measured. The poor girl needed her rest. He'd need to be extra quiet to insure he didn't disturb her slumber.

The Henry was lying on the floor next to her mattress.

Hickok retrieved the long gun and walked outside, squinting in the sun. He sat down on the outside steps and relaxed, enjoying the warm sensation spreading through his limbs. It was too cool in the concrete building.

Maybe he should explore the area? No. Too risky. It would leave Bertha unprotected, helpless.

So what to do?

Something to his right made a loud scratching noise.

Hickok turned his head, scanning. Just the deserted street and dozens of vacant, worn buildings.

Probably an animal of some sort.

The scratching came again. Sounded like metal on metal.

Hickok warily stood, raising the Henry. What now? One of the things Geronimo had shot earlier?

There it was again!

Hickok moved cautiously along the cracked sidewalk, listening. He didn't like this one bit. The instinct he relied upon to alert him to danger was acting up, shrieking in his brain.

This time he pinpointed the sound. It was emanating from a frame house half a block away.

Hickok glanced back at the concrete building. No sign of anyone trying to sneak up on him or get inside. Whoever, or whatever, was in front of him, luring him with the noises, wanted him.

Well, they'd sure as blazes get him!

His eyes alertly covering every inch of the surrounding vicinity, Hickok, expecting an ambush at any second, reached the walk leading up to the frame house.

The scratching had ceased.

To be expected.

Hickok moved toward the gaping doorway. There was no sign of a door. The interior of the house was dark and forbidding. He stopped, debating. His common sense told him to return to the concrete building and wait for the others to come back.

The soft scraping above him forewarned him, too late, of the attack.

Hickok was bringing the Henry up, his eyes darting toward the opening on the second floor where a window pane had existed at one time.

Blast!

The first attacker had already launched himself from the opening, his body slamming into Hickok's, and they both went down hard. The Henry rolled off in the grass.

Hickok twisted, bringing his right knee up, savagely driving it into his attacker's groin area. His assailant, a young man with brown hair and a skimpy beard, gasped and rolled away.

Rising swiftly, Hickok aimed a kick at the man's head, a kick that never landed.

The second attacker came around the corner of the frame house, running and diving and catching Hickok around the legs with both arms.

Hickok hit the walk, pain searing his left shoulder. He swung his left fist, catching the second assailant on the side of his head, above the ear. The man grunted and tried to rise to his knees. Hickok drew in his legs and drove them straight out, striking the man in the chest, flinging him aside. He reached for his right Python.

The first attacker was already up, lunging. He grabbed Hickok's right arm and held it fast. "Get him!" he screamed. "Hurry!"

The second man, a blond with a burly build, scrambled to his feet and moved in. "Hold him!" he urgently directed.

Hickok couldn't free his right arm. The first attacker was clinging to him for dear life. Out of the corner of his left eye he saw the second assailant close in, and he waited until the man was right on top of him before he acted. He swept his left foot up, catching the man in the shins, causing him to stumble and trip over his own feet. The blond sprawled on the walk, cursing.

"I'm losing my grip!" skimpy beard warned. "Help me!"

Hickok, furious, extended the first two fingers of his left hand, held them rigid, and stabbed them directly into the first attacker's right eye.

Skimpy beard screeched in agony and released his hold on Hickok's right arm.

Hickok jumped to his feet, reaching for the right Python again.

"Not this time!" came from the blond.

Hickok spun, the right Colt clearing leather.

Not fast enough.

The blond had grabbed a huge chunk of broken walk, a jagged piece of cement, and flung it with all his strength at the gunman.

Hickok tried to duck, to dodge the projectile, but the heavy cement caught him above his right eye, tearing the flesh, blood pouring out, stunning him momentarily.

The blond, seeing his temporary advantage, closed in. He swung his bony fists twice, pounding the gunman on the chin, staggering him. A final blow to the side of the head brought him down.

The blond stared at the fallen gunman, catching his breath. "Whew! He was one tough son of a bitch!"

"You and your bright ideas, Harry." The younger man rose to his feet, holding his right hand over his right eye. "The bastard almost took out my eye!"

"If he'd been able to bring those guns into play," Harry commented, "I have a feeling we wouldn't be alive right now."

"But we are," skimpy beard verified, "and we've got to get him back."

"I don't know . . ." Harry hesitated.

"What the hell do you mean by that?" the younger man bitterly demanded. "Catching one of them alive was your idea! Well, we've done it. So let's get this sucker out of here before any more of them show up."

Harry glanced back down the street, toward the concrete building. "No sign of anyone else. Maybe he was the only one left behind when the others drove off."

"We can't take that chance."

"All right, Pete. I wonder what happened to Joe and the rest."

"I have an idea," Pete replied, staring coldly at Hickok.

"Let's tie him up and get out of here," Harry suggested.

Pete reached into his pants pockets and removed a length of cord. He knelt and securely tied Hickok's arms behind his back. "I'll take these," he announced, and unbuckled Hickok's gun belt and strapped it around his own lean waist. He picked up the right Colt and slid it into his holster.

"Then I get the rifle." Harry spotted the Henry in the tall grass and claimed it as his own.

"This was your idea," Pete stressed again. "I agree that the general will want to question this man. But I don't expect this guy to come along peacefully. He'll make trouble for us, for sure."

"That will just be too bad for him," Harry snapped, rubbing his sore chest.

"How do you mean?"

"If this bastard gives us too much trouble," Harry promised, "I'll personally blow his brains out."

9

The SEAL came to a stop in front of the concrete building.

"No sign of anyone," Geronimo commented. "Maybe we should stay out here for a while."

"Why?" Joshua asked.

Geronimo smirked. "We wouldn't want to interrupt Hickok and Bertha if they're getting acquainted, would we?"

"Surely they wouldn't!" Joshua exclaimed.

Geronimo laughed. "You don't know Hickok like I know Hickok. He's capable of anything."

Blade opened his door. "He better be on guard duty."

They followed one another into the building. Bertha was sleeping, curled up on her right side.

"No sign of Nathan," Joshua observed.

"Strange," Blade noted. "Geronimo, check upstairs. Joshua, the basement."

Blade turned and searched outside, surveying the street and the park. No sign of his friend.

"He's not upstairs," Geronimo said, returning.

A moment later Joshua came up from the basement. He approached them, shaking his head.

"Where could he be?" Geronimo asked.

"Maybe he's in the park relieving himself," Blade suggested.

They waited, hoping Hickok would emerge from the park, their anxiety building.

"Would he be hiding somewhere?" Joshua asked.

"He may have his faults," Blade replied, "but being childish isn't one of them."

"I have an idea," Geronimo offered.

"What?" Blade asked him.

"I saw a trap door in the hallway upstairs. Must be the way to get to the roof. Why don't I climb up there and look around? It'd be a great vantage point."

Blade nodded. "Go to it."

Geronimo ran up the stairs.

Blade walked over to Bertha, knelt, and gently shook her.

"Leave me alone," she sleepily mumbled.

Blade shook her shoulder until she opened her eyes.

"What is it?" she drowsily inquired.

"Have you seen Hickok? We can't find him."

This woke her up. "White Meat? No. Last I knew, he was sitting right next to me. Where could he be?"

"Don't know."

"I don't like this," Blade said, standing. He walked to the door and leaned against the jamb.

Bertha threw her blanket to one side and stood.

"You shouldn't be doing that," Joshua told her.

"I can manage," she responded. She shuffled forward and joined Blade. "You think something happened to him?"

"It's not like him to disappear," Blade said. "He's one of the most reliable people I know."

"Says a lot for his character."

Blade smiled at Bertha.

"Surely, if Hickok had been attacked, Bertha would have heard something," Joshua commented.

"I'm a pretty heavy sleeper," Bertha stated.

"Well," Joshua said, persisting with his train of thought, "if someone attacked Hickok, surely they would have also attacked you."

"Who can say?" Bertha answered. "Maybe they was tooty-fruity and just wanted him."

"Tooty-fruity?" Joshua asked, puzzled.

"Gay."

"What does being happy have to do with this situation?"

Bertha appeared surprised by Joshua's statement. "Don't you know what I mean? Maybe they were faggots."

Joshua's confused expression denoted his lack of comprehension.

"Lordy, you sure are a babe in the woods, ain't you?" Bertha snapped, exasperated. "Maybe they liked men! Get it?"

"You mean . . . sexually?" Joshua asked, horrified.

"It's been known to happen, Josh, my man," Bertha informed him.

"I've never known any man who was that . . . way," Joshua said.

"Yes, you have," Blade told him.

"I have?" Joshua faced Blade. "Who?"

"Our good and former friend, Joe the Watcher."

"How do you know?" Joshua asked skeptically.

"He told us," Blade replied. "He told us he wanted you, and he intended to have you after they disposed of the rest of us."

Joshua's face visibly paled. "I had no idea," he absently mumbled.

"You're learning, though," Blade noted.

There was a loud thumping sound from upstairs,

followed by the pounding of feet on the hallway
floor. Geronimo appeared at the top of the stairs.

"Code One!" Geronimo yelled. "The SEAL!"

The Family Warriors had developed a system of
verbal and sign signals designed to convey
warnings, signals, and other information. A low
whistle meant danger, take cover. Code One told
other Warriors a critical emergency situation
existed, requiring immediate action and
compliance with no questions asked.

"Move!" Blade ordered as Geronimo came down
the stairs.

"What's going on, babe?" Bertha asked,
alarmed.

Joshua was staring vacantly at the floor.

"Get in the SEAL!" Blade shoved Joshua
toward the door.

"What . . . ?" Joshua began, and was immediately cut off.

"Get in the SEAL!" Blade shouted. He grabbed
Bertha's left arm and drew her out the doorway
and to the SEAL.

Geronimo joined them, opening the SEAL's door
on the passenger side.

Joshua climbed in, then helped pull Bertha up
onto the rear seat with him. They perched there,
obviously confused.

Geronimo climbed into the front.

Blade ran around the SEAL and jumped in the
driver's seat.

"Which way?" Blade asked Geronimo.

"Turn it around," Geronimo directed. "Head
south."

Blade started the engine, threw the transmission
into drive, and wheeled the SEAL in a tight
U-turn. He followed the street along the park until
they came to a wide avenue bearing south. Blade
turned onto the avenue and gunned the motor.

"Will someone tell me what the hell is going on?"
Bertha angrily demanded. "I got a right to know."

"I was on the roof," Geronimo explained. "I saw
three men heading south, and one of them had his
hands tied behind his back. It was Hickok."

Bertha anxiously leaned forward. "You sure?"

"Positive," Geronimo stated. "The distance was
too great to make out much detail, but from the
way Hickok was moving I'd say he's been
injured."

"Oh no!" Bertha gripped Blade's shoulder. "Go
faster, man! Move this thing!"

"What do you think I'm doing?" Blade retorted.

The SEAL was moving at fifty miles per hour,
the fastest Blade could push it on streets clogged
with fallen debris and litter, the transport weaving
sharply to avoid each obstacle.

"How far were they?" Blade asked Geronimo.

"A dozen city blocks when I spotted them."

"Then we should overtake them easily," Blade
said confidently.

"Maybe not," Geronimo said.

"Why?"

"They were making for a line of trees that runs
from near where I saw them all the way to the edge
of Thief River Falls. If they do reach those trees,
they'll have cover all the way out of town. They
obviously know this area pretty well."

"Damn!" Blade snapped, frustrated. "We've got
to beat them to those trees!"

They didn't.

Blade, following Geronimo's directions, reached
the street paralleling the trees. There was no sign
of Hickok or his captors.

"Those trees are bordering a stream," Joshua
stated, spotting the water, lurching in his seat as
Blade abruptly braked the SEAL.

"They could easily hide their trail by using the

stream," Geronimo mentioned. "They're trying to lose any possible pursuit. These guys are pros."

"Go!" Blade urged. "We'll catch up."

"My Browning," Geronimo said, turning in his seat and reaching back.

Joshua picked the shotgun up from the rear section and passed it to Geronimo.

"Silent stalk," Blade advised as Geronimo opened his door and leaped out.

Geronimo nodded grimly, once, and ran off, making for the line of trees. The greenbelt averaged a hundred yards in width.

"On second thought," Blade said to the others, watching Geronimo vanish in the vegetation, "you two will stay put until we return."

"I ain't stayin' here," Bertha argued.

Blade turned to her. "You'll do what I tell you," he informed her harshly, "when I tell you, for as long as you stay with us. I can't leave the SEAL unattended."

Bertha went to speak again.

"I've got no time to mince words." Blade pounded the top of his bucket seat. "Stay here with Joshua until we get back. Give me the Commando," he said to Joshua.

Joshua meekly complied. "Take care."

Blade threw his door open and climbed out. He paused for one look back. "If we don't return in one day," he ordered, "take the SEAL and go back to the Home." He spun and ran toward the trees.

"That sucker don't beat around the bush," Bertha said as they saw Blade follow Geronimo's path into the greenbelt.

"He's accustomed to being obeyed in times of crisis," Joshua explained. "He's a Triad leader, after all."

"I think I can see why," was all Bertha would say.

Joshua bent his head in prayer.

10

"Move your ass, damnit!" Harry shoved Hickok, who stumbled and nearly fell.

"Take it easy," Pete suggested. "He's still weak from the bash on the head, and he's lost an awful lot of blood."

"Who cares?" Harry rejoined. "If he can't keep up, he'll be losing more blood, right quick."

"What's your big rush?"

They were moving down the center of a small stream, the water only six inches deep. Dense brush and trees closed in on the stream.

"I don't want any of his friends catching up with us," Harry said, casting a nervous glance over his shoulder.

"Fat chance. We've got too big a head start." Pete stepped over a rock. He was leading, Hickok in the middle, Harry bringing up the rear.

"Maybe," Harry said doubtfully. He had his Winchester 70 XTR 30-06 slung over his left shoulder and was carrying the Henry.

Pete had the Pythons around his waist, and he was toting a Springfield Armory M1A rifle. "So what if they do catch us?" He tried to assure

Harry. "We'll just blow 'em away."

"Oh?" Harry shook his head. The kid sure was green behind the ears. "Don't forget. They wasted Joe and the others. I don't want to tangle with them unless we've got no other choice."

Joe had been one of the best fighters Pete knew, and Bert the fastest gunman. Pete held his Springfield tighter, alert now for any movement or sound.

Hickok slipped on a stone and fell to his knees.

"Get up!" Harry hauled him to his feet. "You drop again and you'll never be getting up!"

Hickok moved weakly ahead, his legs sluggish. This is another fine mess you've gotten yourself into, he thought. His head felt like it was splitting open, and the gash above his right eye was throbbing painfully. What the blazes should he do now? He was certain his friends would not find him. Harry and Pete had kept to the walks until they entered the trees, and not even Geronimo could track on cement. So his escape was entirely up to him. But what to do? He was too weak to engage them in unarmed combat, and they had his guns. His guns! He stared longingly at the Colts Pete was wearing. If he could just get his hands on one of them . . .

"Speed it up!" Harry pushed Hickok. "You've moving too damn slow!"

You'll be getting yours, brother! You'll be getting yours! Hickok tried to loosen his wrists again, to no avail. Whoever had tied him had done a good job. His circulation was cut off, his fingers becoming numb.

"Should we stop and rest?" Pete asked.

"Not until we've put the town miles behind us," Harry replied.

What options were left? Making a run for it? In his condition? Hickok surreptitiously studied the growth along the stream. The brush was heavy, packed with thick weeds, providing abundant hiding places. His best bet.

They marched on, the sun climbing well up in the western sky.

"I'm getting tired," Pete complained.

"Just keep moving," Harry said wearily.

"But we haven't had any rest since yesterday morning," Pete whined. "First we're sent out on patrol. We come back a day later and find our buddies have apparently been killed. You decide to capture one and take him to the general. I don't mind telling you, I'm beat."

"I'll beat you if you don't shut up and keep moving," Harry growled. "We'll stop when I say we stop and not before. You were trained for this, just like the rest of us. The best training you could ever get. Remember, Samuel is counting on us."

Pete sighed. "So they say."

"Watch your mouth!" Harry exploded. "Some might call that treason! Do you want to go on report when we get back?"

Pete, obviously shaken, shook his head. "Nope. Sure don't."

"That's the trouble with this extended field duty," Harry muttered. "Discipline goes all to hell."

"I'm sorry, sergeant," Pete quickly apologized. "I really am. I didn't mean anything by it."

"I understand, kid," Harry said. "We haven't been back in a year. Good thing we're due for relief real soon."

Pete had a thought. "Say, why didn't we wait for a chance to sneak in and get the transmitter? We could have called for help."

Hickok's interest perked up.

"What the blazes was this? They talked like they were some sort of military men! Impossible! But why'd the bearded one call the other sergeant?

Why weren't they wearing uniforms, instead of jeans and shirts? What was this about a transmitter?

"Too risky," Harry was saying. "I doubt they found the transmitter in its hiding place, but we'd still be taking too big a chance trying to sneak inside and get it. If we were caught, not only would we have failed in our assignment, but they would have one of our transmitters. They might just figure out what's going on."

"Naw," Pete disagreed. "No way. None of these creeps is that smart."

"Don't underestimate them, Pete," Harry advised. "Don't ever underestimate them."

They walked in silence for a spell.

Hickok, despite his extreme fatigue and discomfort, was racking his brain for an out. There had to be a way to escape! He had valuable information to get back to Blade. There was more to these Watchers than anyone had guessed.

The stream curved ahead, the bend littered with small stones and pebbles lodged there by periodic heavy rainfall. To their right, a ragged ravine cut into the trees. The ravine was packed with growth and cluttered with large boulders.

Hickok scanned the mouth of the ravine. If he could reach it and plunge into the dense undergrowth, he just might be able to follow the ravine to safety. But how should he make the break? There was only one way. He might end up with a bullet in his head, but he had no other choice. The longer they marched, the weaker he would become. He had to act now, while he still had some strength remaining.

Pete rounded the curve.

Hickok deliberately slowed, moving his feet at a shuffle, weaving.

"How many times I gotta tell you?" Harry demanded. "Move your ass!" He used the stock of the Henry and jabbed Hickok between the shoulder blades.

Hickok pretended to trip and fall to his knees.

"Damn you!" Harry angrily roared. "Don't give out on us now! We've still got a ways to go."

Pete had slowed and was looking back over his left shoulder. "Can we stop now?" he hopefully asked.

"No!" Harry approached Hickok on his right side. "What the hell is the matter with you? Did that conk on the head do some internal damage?"

Hickok sagged, refusing to answer. He needed Harry to move around in front of him, to place his stocky body between Pete and the ravine, to reduce Pete's line of fire with that Springfield.

Harry thumped Hickok on the right shoulder. "Get up, you son of a bitch, or I'll finish you right now."

Hickok groaned.

Pete had stopped twenty yards away. "Can't you see he's exhausted?"

"He'll be dead if he doesn't move!"

Hickok bent over at the waist, his head almost touching the water. He gathered his energy, his leg muscles tightening. Come on, blast you! Move around in front!

"Okay, sucker. I warned you." Harry stepped in front of Hickok and raised the Henry.

"Wait!" Pete yelled.

"Why?"

"Won't the shot carry for miles?"

Harry nodded, understanding. His anger had nearly gotten the better of him. If he fired the rifle, the friends of this buckskin-clad fool might hear and come running.

"I'll make it quiet," Harry promised. He lowered the Henry and reached for a large hunting knife held in a sheath on his left hip. "I'll slice him from ear to ear." He grinned.

It was now or never!

Hickok surged upward, ramming his right shoulder into Harry, knocking the man aside, his arms and legs flapping as he tried to recover his balance.

"Harry!" Pete exclaimed. He jerked the Springfield to his shoulder, prepared to fire, but Harry was between him and the prisoner.

Hickok darted into the ravine, head first, the underbrush grabbing at his body, barbed limbs tearing at his exposed face. He disappeared, the thicket closing behind him.

"Son of a bitch!" Harry fumed, enraged. He had regained his footing as Hickok vanished, and brought the Henry up, too late to fire.

"What do we do?" Pete ran back and joined his companion. "Let him get away?"

"Like hell!" Harry spat into the water. "We kill him, that's what we do. Don't worry about the noise either. We'll be long gone by the time any help could arrive."

"What then?"

"You take the left bank," Harry said, pointing at the sloping southern ridge of the ravine, "and I'll take the right. We're bound to find him. When you do, shoot to kill."

"Maybe we can catch him in a cross fire."

"Just so we catch him! Move!"

Pete scrambled up the left ridge, fighting the thick vegetation every step of the way.

Harry did likewise on the northern slope.

Pete reached the top and crouched, his eyes probing for any sign. The brush below was quiet, undisturbed by human passage. Locating their captive would be difficult. He could hide in dozens of places, wait for them to pass him by, then backtrack to the stream and make his escape.

Harry stopped at the top of the other ridge, getting his bearings. He could see Pete searching for the target. Where the hell was he? Harry moved along the ridge, avoiding the trees and boulders blocking his way. He skirted the thickest brush, always keeping to the ravine side, seeking his quarry. Those buckskins shouldn't be too hard to spot, even with the growth as bad as it was. All it would take would be just one revealing shaft of sunlight.

Ahead, a bird twittered. The call was answered by another bird on Pete's ridge.

Harry stepped carefully, minimizing his noise. He noticed three large boulders down in the ravine, arranged in a naturally shaped triangle, with a small space between them. A space big enough for a man? It would make excellent cover and ideal protection from shots fired from the ridges. If I were hiding down there, Harry told himself, that's where I would go to ground. He stopped next to a tree and crouched, biding his time. Sooner or later that bastard would show himself.

There was no sign of Pete.

Harry shifted his weight from his left to his right leg. The left was beginning to cramp. He was sick and tired of this field duty! He wanted to get home, back to civilization, where he belonged.

There was a soft scuffing sound behind him.

Harry casually turned his head, not expecting any trouble, knowing the prisoner couldn't possibly have climbed the walls of the ravine in his condition. So he was completely startled to see a man in green, with brown eyes and short black hair, standing four feet away, holding a hatchet or something similar over his head.

"Pete!" Harry screamed, pivoting, bringing the Henry to bear.

Geronimo, one of his tomahawks upraised, leaped, hitting the Watcher square in the chest, bowling him over, both of them tumbling down the ravine.

Pete, on the opposite ridge, heard Harry's warning shout. He ran as quickly as he could, trying to spot Harry. Damn it! Why had he let Harry get out of sight? He spied a commotion on the slope of the northern ridge.

Harry was fighting another man!

Pete hurried, hunting for an open spot, needing a clear shot if he was to come to Harry's assistance. He found a level spot below a boulder and stopped, raising the Springfield to his shoulder. Come on, Harry! Give me a shot!

Harry had lost his rifle. He was grappling with a man in green, the two rolling in the brush. Harry clutched his hunting knife in his left hand, and his attacker held something resembling a hatchet in his right. Both men strained, trying to gain the advantage.

Come on, Harry!

"Drop the gun!"

The voice came from behind and above him.

Pete instinctively ducked and swung the Springfield, cursing his stupidity for not realizing there might be another attacker.

This new menace was perched on top of the boulder, a muscular man with a large knife in his right hand.

Pete got off a hasty shot, knowing he had missed, watching in horror as the man made an overhand motion. He caught the gleam of the streaking blade, and a shock struck his chest as it entered.

"No!" Pete managed a croak, his limbs sagging as he gaped at the knife handle protruding from his chest. "It can't be," he added, losing his grip on the Springfield. It fell to the ground, and a moment later he followed it.

Blade jumped from the boulder, landing beside his fallen foe. "You really should have dropped the gun," he said.

The struggle on the other slope was intensifying.

Harry freed his knife hand and lunged, missing. He was lying on the bottom, with the other man's right knee pressed into his stomach.

"Drop the knife," Geronimo ordered. Blade had said they should try to take one of these men alive, if at all possible.

"Go to hell!" Harry hissed, swinging the knife again, missing again.

Geronimo wrenched his right arm free and slashed the tomahawk straight down, the blade biting into Harry's forehead, driving deep.

Harry's eyes widened, he gasped for air, his limbs thrashing, and he tried to rise.

Geronimo stood and watched the Watcher's death throes. "You can go to hell," he stated as Harry died. "When I go, I'm going to the higher worlds of the Great Spirit."

"You all right?" Blade called from the other ridge.

"Fine. How about you?"

"Okay. Where do you think Hickok is?"

"Right here." Hickok was standing between three boulders in the ravine blow. He seemed to be having difficulty staying on his feet.

Blade and Geronimo moved toward Hickok.

"You hurt?" Blade asked the gunman. He noticed Hickok's hands were tied behind his back, his buckskins were streaked with dirt and grime, and his face appeared to be badly battered. There was a prominent wound above his right eyebrow.

"I'm plumb tuckered out, pard," Hickok said feebly as his two friends approached. He began to sway. "As far as being hurt is concerned." He grinned weakly. "I'd have to say . . . the . . . answer . . . is yes."

Hickok's eyes closed and he fell, bouncing off one of the boulders before he hit the ground.

"Nathan!" Blade shouted, racing toward the boulders. Please, he prayed to the Spirit, please let him be alive!

11

"Josh, wake up!" Bertha smacked his left arm. "You've been sleepin' long enough."

Joshua raised his head and opened his eyes. "I'm not sleeping," he informed her.

"Then what've you been doing all this time?"

"Praying."

"Say what?"

"Praying. Don't you know what praying is?" Bertha shook her head.

"What kind of religion do you practice in the Twin Cities?" Joshua inquired.

"Religion? Oh, you mean the God stick."

"The God stick?"

"Yeah." Bertha nervously scanned the trees for the hundredth time since Blade and Geronimo had gone after Hickok. "The Horns do something called the God stick. Never did understand it myself, but then I was born a Porn and I would of died a Porn if I hadn't met Zahner and been convinced to switch to the Nomads."

Joshua, bewildered, pressed her for additional information. "Can you tell me anything about the God stick?"

"Not much. It's one of the big differences between the Horns and the Porns. Has something to do with magic, I think."

"Magic?"

"Yeah. Some mumbo-jumbo about askin' this God for things you want. Sounds crazy, right?"

Joshua was trying to understand. "The Porns don't believe in God?"

Bertha studied him to be sure the question was in earnest. "Are you nuts? Of course they don't. How can you believe in somethin' you can't see or touch or taste? That's what this God bozo is, some kind of invisible thing. Imagine that!" She laughed.

"How do the Nomads feel about God?"

"The Nomads is made up of former Porns and Horns for the most part. Some of 'em believe in the God nonsense, the ones who used to be Horns. The Porns don't, of course."

"Of course."

Bertha fidgeted in her seat. They had climbed into the front seats after Blade departed. She glanced at Joshua. "What are you thinkin' about?" she asked him.

"What you just told me," he replied. "I find it incredible that people could exist and not accept the reality of a Supreme Creator."

"What?"

"I believe in God."

"You do?" Bertha showed her surprise.

"Yes, I do. As a matter of fact, I was talking to God before you hit me on the arm."

Bertha appeared startled. She quickly looked around the interior of the SEAL. "You was talkin' to God?"

"Yes."

"God's in here with us, right this minute?" She bent and peered under her bucket seat.

"Of course."

Bertha sat up, grinning. "You're jive-talkin' me, right?"

"I beg your pardon."

"You're puttin' me on, Josh? Aren't you?"

"No. I'm completely serious."

"Uh-huh," Bertha said slowly. "I can't see no God in this thing. Where is it?"

"Right here." Joshua reached up with his right hand and touched his forehead.

"What?" Bertha nearly screeched. "You tryin' to tell old Bertha that God is you?"

"No," Joshua patiently answered. "I'm simply saying that God is inside of me."

"Don't it get kind of crowded in there?" Bertha cackled.

"You don't believe me?" Joshua asked.

"Do I look like an idiot?"

Joshua smiled. "I'll try to explain."

"Please do. I've been tryin' to understand this God business for a long time."

"God is spirit," Joshua began, and was promptly interrupted.

"What's spirit?" Bertha demanded. She placed her elbows on her knees and rested her chin in her hands.

"Spirit is a level of reality existing on a plane other than the material."

Bertha made a face. "Can't you use a language we both can talk in? I don't understand this at all."

Johsua sighed. He touched his leg. "This body is called material. It's part of what's called physical reality . . ."

"Cute body too," Bertha interjected. "Not as pretty as White Meat, but cute. You got skinny legs, though."

"How am I supposed to tell you about God," Joshua wanted to know, "if you won't let me finish a sentence?"

"I'm all ears."

"Okay."

"I won't break in again."

"Okay. Now . . ."

"I promise."

Joshua shook his head, grinning, and rolled his eyes skyward.

"You feelin' sick?" Bertha asked.

"No. Now can we finish our talk about God?"

"You ain't said nothing yet," Bertha pointed out.

"I'm trying."

"Well, don't let me stop you."

Joshua mentally counted to ten.

"Any time," Bertha said eagerly.

"As I was saying," Joshua continued, "our bodies are called material. We live in a physical, material world. Everything we see and touch and smell is part of this material world."

"I got that," Bertha said proudly.

"There is also another level of reality we can't see or touch or smell. It's called the spiritual level, or spiritual world."

"And where's it at?"

"Right here. All around us. But we can't see it."

"Then how do we know it's there?"

"By feeling it in our lives."

"I just don't get it," Bertha snapped, annoyed at her own lack of comprehension. "How can we feel it if we can't even see it?"

"We feel it here." Joshua touched his forehead again. "When we talk to God, who is spirit, we feel it inside our heads. We can actually feel the presence of God, and the more we talk to God, the more we feel the presence of God."

"Sometimes," Bertha said hesitantly, "when I'm all by my lonesome, thinkin', I do feel something in my head. Could it be God?"

"You need to be talking directly to God to feel God."

"How do I talk to God?"

"The same way you talk to me."

"Come again?"

"You talk to God exactly the same way you talk to me," Joshua explained. "Just remember God is inside your head. The Spirit dwells in every man and woman, every child, on this entire planet. You can talk to the Spirit, but first you must open the door to your mind."

Bertha frowned. "I'm tryin', Josh, but I can't say as I understand much of this. Z tried tellin' me about God a couple of times, but it was no good then too."

"Zahner believes in God?" Joshua asked her.

"Of course. Z used to be a Horn before he started the Nomads."

"Of course."

Bertha stretched. "All this talkin' is hurtin' my head. I think I'll take a walk and clear the cobwebs."

"Wouldn't it be safer to remain in the SEAL?" Joshua anxiously inquired.

"Safer maybe," Bertha admitted. "But I need some fresh air. Your friends have been gone a long time." She opened her door.

Joshua reached into the back of the SEAL and picked up the Smith and Wesson Pump shotgun. "Here. If you insist on going outside, the least you can do it take adequate protection."

Bertha happily took the gun. "Ain't this a beaut!" she exclaimed, admiring the firearm. "I wish I'd of had one of these back in the Twins! I wouldn't have worried about nothing."

Joshua stayed in the SEAL, nervously scanning the trees and the nearest buildings. He didn't like the idea of her leaving the safety of the transport. There was no telling what might be out there. More Watchers, Mutates. Or more like the thing that attacked Blade near the park.

The sun was high in the sky, white clouds floating lazily overhead. Four robins were half a block away, searching for worms and insects in a patch of grass.

It looked harmless enough.

Bertha had moved nearer the trees. She was holding the shotgun loosely in her hands, gazing at the wall of vegetation.

Joshua closed his eyes and concentrated, mentally probing, seeking any fluctuations, any disruptive patterns in their immediate area, utilizing his empathic ability as Hazel had taught him to do, trying to perceive the emanation of hostile emotions.

"Hey, Josh!" Bertha called, turning her back to the trees. "It's beautiful out here! Why don't you join me?"

Joshua felt . . . something . . . touch his mind, something primitive, something elemental, something savage.

"Come on, Josh!" Bertha urged him. "Don't worry! I'll guard you, keep you safe from the boogeyman!" She laughed, her back still to the trees.

Joshua opened his eyes, terrified, reaching for the doorknob, knowing he had to warn her, to get Bertha back to the SEAL. Even as he opened the door, he saw the leafy green foliage behind Bertha part, revealing a hideous, leering dark face with a countenance straight from his worst possible nightmare.

"Come on!" Bertha waved to him.

Joshua's feet touched the ground, his eyes widening as the creature stepped in view. Dear

Father! No! It was a female version of the brute
that had assaulted Blade, start naked except for a
skimpy piece of buckskin around the waist,
covering her private parts. It had the same big
nose, and the same huge mouth, open now,
revealing two rows of sharp, jagged teeth. The
heavy body was blackish, rough, displaying dozens
and dozens of scars. Two immense, pendulous
breasts swayed as the creature walked toward
Bertha!

"What's the matter, Josh?" Bertha asked,
noting his expression.

Joshua started to bring his hand up, to point, at
a loss for words.

Bertha crouched, spinning, the Smith and
Wesson up and ready. Too late.

The thing was already directly behind Bertha,
calmly standing there, apparently studying her.

"Look out!" Joshua finally screamed.

The brute lashed out, its right arm knocking the
shotgun to the ground. Before Bertha could
recover, the creature struck with its left arm,
catching Bertha on the side of the head.

"Bertha!" Joshua shouted, taking a few steps in
her direction. What should he do? Try to distract
the thing, make it come after him?

Bertha was lying on the ground, groaning. The
shotgun was out of her reach.

The female brute stood over Bertha, watching
her, saliva dripping out of the corners of the
cavernous mouth.

Joshua waved his arms, frantically striving to
distract the thing. "Here! Over here! Leave her
alone!" Maybe, if he could draw the creature away
from Bertha, Bertha might be able to get the
shotgun and shoot the brute.

"Try me! Leave her alone!" Joshua yelled.

The creature ignored him, kneeling, reaching

down to touch Bertha's hair.

"Leave her alone!"

The brute looked up at Joshua, annoyed by the noise.

"Over here, you monstrosity!"

The thing decided Joshua wasn't much of a threat and returned its attention to Bertha.

Bertha's eyes flickered open. "What the hell . . ."

The brute growled, the long fangs exposed.

Bertha tried to rise.

The creature slammed her to the ground with its left hand, then placed that hand on Bertha's chest, pressing down, preventing Bertha from rising.

"Let me up!" Bertha screamed, furious. "Let me up, you ugly bitch!"

The brute hissed and cuffed Bertha with its right hand.

"Joshua!" Bertha shrieked. "Joshua? Help me!"

Joshua wavered, his mind racing. What should he do? If he went any closer, the thing would get him too. He had to stop the creature! But how?

"Joshua!" Bertha screeched, her voice breaking. "Where the hell are you?"

The brute, growling, picked up Bertha's left arm with its right hand and raised the arm to its face.

Dear Father! What is the thing doing?

The creature was sniffing, running Bertha's arm under its bent nose.

No! No! It couldn't be! Joshua suddenly perceived what was coming.

The thing opened his mouth, wide, and bit down on Bertha's arm.

Bertha screamed, twisting and turning, trying to break free.

The brute held the left arm in its mouth, blood dripping over its chin, the jaws slowly working.

Dear Father! It was eating Bertha!

"Joshua!" Bertha was hysterical now. "Save me!"

What do I do? Kill the thing? Could he do it? The brute appeared to be slightly human. How could he morally condone killing the creature if there was the slightest possibility that it was endowed with a minimal spiritual capacity?

The thing was licking Bertha's arm, savoring the tangy taste of blood and flesh.

"Joshua!"

Joshua, wild with anxiety, frenziedly searched for anything nearby he could use as a weapon. A rock. A limb. Anything.

Nothing.

"Joshua!" Bertha renewed her feeble efforts to break loose.

Joshua ran toward them, then stopped. The shotgun was too close to the brute. If he tried to grab it, the thing would nail him.

Dear Father!

"Joshua! Joshua, *please!*"

Were there any guns left in the SEAL? Joshua dashed to the transport and jumped in. The Warriors had taken their firearms with them, and the rest of the confiscated weapons were hidden at the edge of town.

Bertha was sobbing and thrashing as the brute gnawed on her arm.

Joshua couldn't stand to look! He glanced down, at the foor behind the driver's bucket seat.

A gun!

The Ruger Redhawk he had dropped on the floor, the gun they'd taken from the motorcycle rider who'd tried to kill them!

"Joshua!" Bertha wailed pitiably.

Joshua leaned down and scooped up the Redhawk, flinging his body from the SEAL, running toward the brute and Bertha. Was the gun loaded? There wasn't time to check!

The thing saw him coming and released Bertha, rising.

Joshua stopped, amazed at how tall the creature was.

"Shoot it!" Bertha had twisted onto her side, and was holding her left arm pressed close to her body.

Joshua raised the .44 Magnum and aimed at the thing's face.

The creature hissed, showing a mouth filled with red froth and chunks of dark flesh.

"Shoot it!"

The brute stepped over Bertha, ignoring her, and came toward Joshua.

Joshua could feel his blood pounding in his temples, and he trembled as his finger tightened on the trigger. "Please!" he pleaded. "Don't make me shoot you!"

Bertha struggled to her knees. "Don't talk to the damn thing! Shoot it!"

The creature was only feet away, coming on slowly, confidently, as if sensing Joshua's inner turmoil.

Joshua felt sweat line the palms of his hands as he tried to will his finger to fire the Magnum. "Don't come any closer," he warned the thing.

"*Shoot it!*" Bertha bent over, her head touching the grass, dreading what was coming.

"Please!" Joshua begged one last time.

The brute suddenly roared and lunged for Joshua.

The .44 Magnum fired, the bullet striking the creature in the forehead, bringing it up short, a stunned expression on its horrible face.

"I'm sorry," Joshua said softly.

The Redhawk cracked again, and again.

The thing was slammed backward by the impact, howling as it dropped to the ground, the muscular limbs still twitching.

"I'm so sorry."

Joshua walked up to the brute, placed the barrel against its head, and pulled the trigger.

"May the Spirit forgive me."

Joshua, abruptly weak, sat down on the grass, the Redhawk falling beside him. He couldn't seem to focus his thoughts. What had he just done? Killed another creature! "Thou shalt not kill." Violated one of the Ten Commandments! Rejected every moral and spiritual imperative! He sagged, feeling a need for sleep.

"Don't faint on me, sucker!"

A firm hand gripped Joshua's shoulder and shook him.

"There might be more of them things around. We got to get back to the SEAL!"

Joshua tried to touch Bertha, but his arms wouldn't rise.

"It's okay," she was telling him. "The thing is dead. You did real good."

Joshua nodded. "I did real good," he repeated, mumbling.

"What's the matter with you, Josh?" Bertha asked. "It was it or me. I'm glad you picked me! I was beginning to wonder if you'd ever fire that gun!"

"I killed it," Joshua said numbly.

Bertha stared at the gaping holes in the creature's head. "You sure as hell did!"

"I killed it!"

"Hey? What's wrong? Is this the first time you've ever killed somethin'?"

Joshua nodded.

"Well, don't blame yourself. God had a lot to do with it."

"God?" Joshua gaped at Bertha, uncomprehending.

"Sure enough. When that thing was comin' at you, I thought you weren't ever going to shoot. So

I did like you told me. I talked to God," she said proudly.

"You talked to God?"

"Yep. I told God I didn't want us ending up as dead meat, and I asked if God would help you fire the gun."

"You did what?" Joshua's head was clearing and he stood.

"You bet. I asked God to make your finger pull the trigger. I talked to God inside my head, just like you said I should."

"You asked God to help me kill?"

"Sure did." Bertha was beaming, despite her pain. "And damn if it didn't work! Maybe there is something to this God business after all!"

Joshua began laughing, an emotional release to the recent events, his mirth uncontrollable.

"What's so funny?" Bertha inquired, trying to understand.

"Nothing," Joshua managed to reply, before the laughter doubled him over.

"I'm sure glad you can laugh while I suffer," Bertha said harshly.

Joshua immediately straightened, the thought of her injury sobering him.

"That's better."

"How bad is it?" he asked, taking her left arm and examining the bite marks.

"I've been hurt worse," she answered. "You know, Josh, White Meat sure was right about you."

"How do you mean?"

"No offense meant," she said, inadvertently flinching when he accidentally touched a tender spot near her wound, "but you are one strange dude!"

"Enjoy it while it lasts."

"What do you mean?"

"I mean," Joshua said, sighing, gazing at the dead brute, "at the rate we're going, by the time this trip is done, I probably won't have much strangeness left in me."

"You'll be normal like the rest of us?" Bertha asked.

"You call yourselves normal?"

12

"I can't get over it!" Hickok laughed uproariously, despite the lancing agony in his head. "I just can't get over it!"

"You've made that abundantly clear," Joshua dryly commented. "I believe we get the picture."

"Old Josh actually blows away one of those critters! Incredible!" Hickok couldn't seem to stop laughing.

"It wasn't so funny for those who were there," Bertha observed stiffly.

"Sorry, Black Beauty," Hickok apologized. "But if you knew Josh like I know Josh, you'd be plumb amazed at him shooting that thing. Say, what are we going to call them disgusting vermin anyway?" he called out to Blade, who was driving the SEAL back to the concrete building in the center of Thief River Falls.

"I don't know what they were," Blade replied.

"They sure were ugly brutes," Bertha stated, frowning.

"Then that's what we'll call them," Blade said.

"What?" Joshua asked. "Ugly? I thought that was the name the people in the Twin Cities used for the mutates."

"It is," Blade confirmed. "No, I mean we'll officially dub the creatures we've encountered the brutes. Has a nice ring to it, don't you think?"

"The brutes?" Geronimo smiled. "It certainly is a scientific title, I'll say that. Plato would be proud of you, Blade."

"Do you think there are any more?" Bertha nervously inquired.

"Probably," Blade admitted. "Whatever the brutes are, I doubt there were just the two we killed in existence. There are bound to be more."

"Where the blazes do they come from?" Hickok wanted to know.

"If I knew that," Blade responded, driving at a sedate pace, "I'd qualify for a position as a Family Empath." He searched for Joshua in the rear-view mirror. "By the way, Joshua, I'm proud of the manner in which you handled yourself during the attack on poor Bertha."

"It wasn't much," Joshua said softly, embarrassed.

"To the contrary," Blade disagreed, "it was a major step for you to take. What pleases me most, though, is that you finally brought your psychic abilities into play. It was about time."

"I require relative quiet and a minimum of distractions to properly focus my mental capabilities," Joshua explained. "Since we left the Home, everything has happened too fast. There's been barely time to catch my breath."

"Well, pard," Hickok spoke up, "don't expect things to change much during the rest of this trip. We seem to attract trouble like horse manure attracts flies."

"You always did have an eloquence with words." Geronimo chuckled.

"We're here," Blade announced, braking the

transport in front of the Watchers' former headquarters and parking at the foot of the front steps.

"So what now?" Bertha questioned.

"We tend to your wounds," Blade replied,
exiting the SEAL, "and hold a conference."

Joshua, over their vociferous objections, forced
Hickok and Bertha to recline on blankets next to
the bar, Bertha on her mattress, Hickok by her
side on the floor. The bites on Bertha's arm were
deep, and some of her flesh had been torn away by
the hungry brute, but the injury wasn't life threat-
ening. Joshua solicitously cleaned the bites, placed
a portion of herbal remedy over the exposed areas,
and bandaged her arm with strips of clean cloth.

"Thanks, Joshua," Bertha said affectionately as
he finished.

"The least I could do," Joshua responded, blushing.

"There you go again." Bertha grinned. "You
must have too much blood in your body, or something."

"Hey!" Hickok interrupted, winking at Bertha.
"Quit your flirting and check me out, okay, pard?"

"I wasn't flirting," Joshua said indignantly. "I
never do."

"You should try it sometime," Hickok recommended. "It's good for what ails you."

"Speaking of which," Joshua retorted, "let's
check and see what's ailing you."

"I can answer that one," Geronimo interjected
from his guard position at the front door. "His
problem is a lack of brains."

Hickok started to speak, but Joshua placed his
left hand over the gunman's mouth. "Be quiet," he
directed. "I can't do this properly if you keep
squirming."

"I should take advantage of this while I have the
chance," Geronimo remarked.

Joshua's gentle fingers probed Hickok's wound above the right eye. "Quite a nasty gash," he said, "and you've lost some blood, but overall, I'd say you're in good shape. Just try to avoid any sudden movements."

"Does that mean he should keep his mouth shut?" Geronimo inquired. "You can actually feel a draft when those lips of his start to fly."

Hickok glared at Geronimo.

"And I wouldn't worry about his injury." Geronimo threw in another zinger for good measure. "Not if it's his head. Whatever they hit him with probably broke."

"That does it," Hickok declared, pushing Joshua aside and rising to his feet. "I'm not a wimp. I'll be all right." He abruptly began swaying and gripped the bar to steady himself.

"I did warn you about sudden movements," Joshua stated.

Blade, seated at the table, finally entered the conversation. "Nathan, lie down," he ordered. "Don't push yourself."

"Yeah, White Meat." Bertha smiled up at him. "Snuggle bunnies with me!"

"We must discuss our next move," Blade advised as Hickok sat on his blanket, "and decide if we head for the Twin Cities in the morning or return to the Home."

"The Home?" Geronimo repeated.

"Your Home?" Bertha said hopefully.

"Bertha," Blade thoughtfully addressed her. "You keep telling us the situation in the Twin Cities is very dangerous . . ."

"You white boys just ain't got no idea what the Twins is like!" Bertha broke in. "They are sheer murder!"

"' . . . so we need to be at optimum effectiveness when we arrive there," Blade said, continuing his train of thought. "Which we are not."

"I can hold my own, pard," Hickok mentioned. "Don't worry none about me."

"I've got to think of all of us," Blade answered. "We must also consider the importance of our mission and the SEAL. I can't see us going into the Twin Cities with Bertha and you at less than your best."

"You mean you're taking me to your Home?" Bertha asked, wonder in her voice.

"I have no choice," Blade replied gruffly. "Besides, look at all the supplies we've taken from the Watchers. The generator is invaluable. We'll dismantle it, load it and all the rest into the back of the transport, and return to our Home. We're not that far. We'll be back by the second day. Give yourselves a week to mend, and we'll be heading for the Twin Cities again. What do you think?" he asked them, glancing around the room.

"Do you need to ask?" Bertha beamed. "I want to reach this Home of yours so bad I can taste it!"

"Whatever you think is best," Geronimo concurred. "You're the leader."

"I think we should continue to the Twins," Hickok protested. "You were hot for the Twin Cities before I was bashed on the noggin. Now you up and change your mind. I get the impression you're changing your mind because of me, and I won't stand for it, pard."

"I admit I want the Healers to examine you," Blade said, sighing, "but you're not the only one hurt." He nodded at Bertha. "What if that arm of hers becomes infected? I just went through such a thing, and it can be real rough. Joshua's medicine bag doesn't contain everything we need to treat a severe infection. Do you want to risk her life because of your pride?"

Hickok glanced at Bertha.

"Oh, please, babe!" she pleaded. "I want to see your Home."

"Well . . ." Hickok shrugged. "If you put it that way," he said to Blade.

Blade smiled, pleased with his persuasiveness. He legitimately was concerned about Hickok's and Bertha's injuries. The Family could use the confiscated supplies and the generator. It was also true a week or two delay would not adversely affect their mission. But, secretly, he nourished an ulterior motive for wanting to return to the Home. He'd felt uneasy leaving with an unidentified power-monger loose in the Family. Plato's assurances to the contrary, no one could guarantee this aspiring despot wouldn't attempt to wrest control of the Family while the Alpha Triad was away. An additional week or two would provide Blade with the time he needed to work on Plato and discover the identity of the traitor.

"If everyone sees the logic," Blade stated, "we'll get a good night's sleep and take off at first light."

"I certainly have a lot to tell my parents," Joshua mentioned. "And I can utilize my time in productive worship to restablish my spiritual equilibrium."

"How long before dark?" Blade asked Geronimo.

Geronimo gazed at the sun. The blazing orb was perched above the western horizon. "Not long," he replied. "I'll take the first watch, if you want."

"Okay." Blade pondered a moment. "Before you do, how about going up on the roof again and scanning the countryside? Make sure our sleep won't be interrupted by unwelcome visitors."

Geronimo took the stairs two at a stride.

"You think there are more Watchers around?" Hickok asked.

"You told us those two said they were on patrol," Blade reminded the gunman. "What if other patrols are still out? What if they come back while we're here?"

"Maybe we should move to another building?" Joshua suggested.

"This one is concrete," Blade noted. "It's in the best shape. The walls are thick, and would provide a sturdy defense against snipers. We've also got the generator. We'll remain here."

"What about that transmitter they mentioned?" Hickok inquired.

"It must be hidden somewhere." Blade looked around the room. "I'll spend every spare moment tonight trying to find it."

"If we can find it," Hickok reasoned, "we can eavesdrop on the Watchers."

"What about the rats?" Joshua questioned.

"We'll take the chance," Blade answered. "It's only for one night."

Hickok eased his body onto his blanket, lying on his back. The cement floor under his blanket was hard and uncomfortable, and intense pain racked his cranium. "I reckon I'm going to nap a spell," he declared. "This head of mine is acting up." He grinned at Bertha and closed his eyes.

"Here," Bertha said. "Use my mattress. It's softer." She stood and stepped aside.

"You sure?" Hickok opened his eyes.

"No problem, White Meat."

"And what are you going to do?" Hickok pushed himself up on his elbows.

"I ain't tired," Bertha stated. "I'll just talk with Blade and Joshua while you get your rest."

"Suit yourself." Hickok shifted onto the mattress and sighed, placing his left arm over his face to block the light. His head was pounding, the temples throbbing.

Bertha walked to the table and sat next to Blade. "You've been straight with me," she said quietly.

"It's only fair I be straight with you."

"About what?" Blade inquired.

"About the Home," Bertha responded.

"What about it?"

Bertha leaned closer to Blade to prevent anyone else from overhearing. "Listen, Blade. If I reach this Home of yours, I ain't ever leaving it. Not ever. Bertha's no dummy. I know a good deal when I see one. If you boys decide later to book to the Twins, you're on your own. I won't go back."

"I appreciate your honesty," Blade remarked.

"I won't go back!" she stressed, her voice rising.

"Is something wrong?" Joshua approached the table.

"Nope." Bertha shook her head, smiling. "For the first time in a long time, everything is all right."

"I don't understand," Joshua admitted.

"Drop it," Bertha advised.

They all heard a loud thump from upstairs, then the sound of someone running.

"Uh-oh!" Bertha said, glancing at the ceiling. "Here we go again!"

Geronimo appeared, moving rapidly down the stairs. "We've got company!" he informed them.

"What?" Blade rose, holding his Commando.

"A convoy," Geronimo stated, making for the doorway.

"A what?" Joshua asked.

"What's going on?" Hickok was standing, his right palm pressed against his temple.

"Four jeeps and a truck," Geronimo explained. "Saw them coming in from the south. Filled with men in green uniforms."

Blade joined Geronimo at the door. "Must be more Watchers," he deduced. "We better make tracks before they arrive."

"We're too late!" Bertha pointed.

Outside, the sun was gone, the last light replaced by the darkening onset of evening. Across the square, on the other side of the park, headlights appeared.

"Listen to those motors!" Joshua remarked. Compared to the raucous noise the jeeps and trucks were producing, the SEAL's prototype engine made a subdued whining sound.

"Do we get out of here?" Hickok said.

"No time," Blade replied. He noticed a switch near Joshua's right shoulder. "Kill the overheads," he ordered.

Joshua flicked the switch down, plunging the interior of the building into gloomy shadow.

"Think they know we're here?" Bertha asked apprehensively.

"If they didn't before," Blade stated, "they do now."

The lead vehicle, a military jeep, screeched to a stop as it rounded the park and its headlights illuminated the SEAL. The rest of the convoy immediately braked. Voices could be heard, commands barked. Figures darted toward the concrete building.

"They're coming this way," Joshus said, delcaring the obvious.

"Quick! The door!" Blade grabbed the door and swung it almost closed, leaving sufficient space to peer out. "There aren't any windows down here," he said. "Geronimo, get upstairs and keep a watch from one of the rooms. Don't let them see you."

"Why don't I use the roof?" Geronimo suggested.

"Go for it," Blade directed. "There aren't any other doors to this building, so they'll need to come in through this one." He spoke his thoughts aloud. "That gives us a certain advantage."

"Did you lock the SEAL?" Hickok asked.

The shapes outside were converging on the transport.

"No!" Blade remembered. "Damn! Stay here!" he told the others, and he was out the door, running for the SEAL, exposed as he covered the dozen steps in front of the building. True night hadn't descended yet, and the twilight revealed eight armed men, all attired in green military uniforms, coming toward the SEAL.

"Waste him!" someone shouted, and the air came alive with the crackle of automatic rifle fire and the buzz of the bullets as they narrowly missed Blade.

"Blade!" Joshua shouted, about to rush outside when a strong hand gripped his left arm and shoved him aside.

Blade felt a slug tear into his right side and he twisted, almost going down, but he regained his footing and stumbled against the transport. He reached for the door as two men appeared, one coming around each end of the SEAL, their guns leveled, their fingers on their triggers.

Hickok suddenly entered the fray, looming tall at the top of the steps, his Pythons already in his hands. The Colts fired, and the two men near Blade collapsed in unison, one of them clutching his head as he fell.

Blade yanked the door open and sprawled inside, closing the door behind him. He reached over and locked the passenger door, then his own. The windows were rolled up. He was protected inside the bulletproof body of the SEAL.

Hickok dodged into the building, a spray of gunfire biting into the concrete wall near his body, narrowly missing him.

Abruptly, all went quiet.

"Whew!" Bertha whispered as they crouched

near the doorway. "That was close!"

"I'm surprised they're not firing at the SEAL," Joshua remarked. "Do you think they know it's bulletproof?"

"Doubt it," Hickok replied. "They probably want the SEAL for themselves," he deduced, "and it wouldn't be too smart to blast it to shreds."

"Think they're more Watchers?" Joshua asked.

"You can bet on it, Joshua my man," Bertha nodded. "I've seen their type before. Some of the Watchers wear uniforms, some of them don't. Beats me why."

From upstairs, from the roof, came the blast of the Browning. Outside, a chorus of automatic fire retaliated.

"Geronimo!" Hickok stated. "What the blazes is he doing?"

"Why don't you go up and ask him, White Meat?" Bertha advised.

"Where's your shotgun?" Hickok inquired, glancing out the door. The Watchers weren't in his line of view.

"By my mattress," Bertha answered.

"Get it," Hickok said. "Can you guard this door while I run upstairs?"

"Can birds fly?" Bertha retorted. She scrambled across the floor, scooped up the Smith and Wesson, and returned.

"Josh, where's your Ruger?" Hickok looked at Joshua.

"I have it on the bar," Joshua responded distastefully.

"Good. If one of those Watchers tries to get in here while I'm on the roof," Hickok told him, "do to them exactly what you did to the brute trying to eat Bertha."

"I don't know if I could," Joshua confessed.

"This is no time to wimp out, pard," Hickok

snapped. "You've finally found your balls. Don't lose 'em now!"

Joshua moved toward the bar.

"Hold tight, Black Beauty," Hickok said to Bertha. He pushed off the floor, grabbed his Henry from near the bar, and ran up the stairs, his eyes adjusted to the dim interior of the building.

Geronimo had placed a stepladder he found in one of the rooms under the trap door, situated in the center of the hallway.

Hickok reached the ladder and carefully climbed to the roof. A cool breeze struck his face as he emerged. The roof was flat, square in shape like the building itself. A foot-high concrete lip ran around the edge of the roof, providing cover for anyone who might need it.

Geronimo was huddled at the front of the roof.

"Don't shoot!" Hickok whispered as he slid forward on his hands and knees. "I know how jumpy you Injuns are!"

"If I'd known it was you," Geronimo rejoined as Hickok reached his side, "I definitely would have shot first and asked questions later."

"What's the layout?" Hickok asked. He cautiously peeked over the concrete lip. Only the lead jeep still had its lights on, focused on the SEAL. The park and the surrounding streets were impenetrable in the darkness.

"When they first came in," Geronimo stated, "I could still see pretty well. There were four Watchers for each jeep, and two more in the cab of the truck. With two dead, that leaves at least sixteen, plus however many were in the back of the truck. Two of the jeeps have machine guns mounted on them. Any idea what type of rifles they're carrying?"

"Think so." Hickok nodded. "They're packing M-16's. We've got two in our armory, and I've fired them a couple of times."

"I wonder what they're up to," Geronimo said. "They're so quiet down there. I spotted one a bit ago and tried to get him, but I think I missed. These guys are professionals."

"They probably won't try anything tonight," Hickok thoughtfully speculated. "They know this area, and particularly this building, very well. After all, they've been using it for who knows how long. A concerted rush on the front door, the only means of entry, would be certain suicide. Especially in the dark." Hickok paused. "I think they'll wait for daylight, then make their move."

"What's to stop them from tossing a grenade in here in the middle of the night?" Geronimo questioned.

"Plenty. These guys might believe we have some of their friends as prisoners. They must also think their supplies are stashed upstairs. How could they possibly know we've moved all their gear? They can't. No, I doubt they'll try anything until morning."

A loud animal roar suddenly rent the night.

"What the blazes . . ." Hickok muttered.

"It came from the park," Geronimo guessed. "Maybe it's a mutate! It could do our job for us."

"Where's the screaming and the gunfire?" Hickok asked doubtfully. "Don't think so. Don't like it either."

"I wish we knew how Blade is doing," Geronimo said, glancing down at the transport. "Why did he run out there anyway? I was on my way up here, and I heard the shooting begin. By the time I reached this spot, Blade was getting into the SEAL. Why?"

"He forgot to lock it," Hickok explained.

"Well," Geronimo reflected aloud, "he should be safe as long as he stays put. Think he'll try to sneak back in here tonight?''

"If he's able.''

"What's that mean?'' Geronimo asked.

"I think he was hit,'' Hickok stated.

"You sure?''

Hickok nodded. "Almost positive. Saw him react like he was struck in the side.''

"And we can't see inside,'' Geronimo remarked.

"Sure can't, pard,'' Hickok said.

"So we have no way of knowing what condition he's in,'' Geronimo reasoned.

"Sure don't,'' Hickok agreed.

"For all we know,'' Geronimo stated apprehensively, "he could be dead.''

"Damn!'' was Hickok's only response.

13

He was fortunate he wasn't dead, Blade mentally told himself as he gingerly felt his right side, immediately below his rib cage, to ascertain the extent of the damage inflicted by the slug. There appeared to be a long furrow, maybe a quarter inch deep, along his side. There was bleeding, but the wound didn't demand prompt treatment. Besides, he had other priorities to consider.

What should he do now?

The bulletproof transport would shield him, but how long could he afford to remain inside the SEAL? The Watchers were undoubtedly concocting their plans for an assault on the building, most likely at dawn. How many were there? What was their firepower? He needed some answers.

What would the Watchers expect him to do? Make a mad dash for the building? Or sit it out in the SEAL? They would have snipers posted to cover the building side of the transport, to cut him down if he did try to get back. But would they have the park side of the SEAL covered?

Blade grinned.

Why should they? The last thing they would

anticipate would be for him to attempt to reach the park. *They* were in the park. They knew he knew he was outnumbered. One man, if he was endowed with any brains, wouldn't conceive of attacking their superior force. It would be the least likely move for anyone with common sense to make.

So he would do it.

Later.

Blade scanned the area. He could distinguish trees and bushes in the park, thanks to the light from the jeep. Were they intending to keep the headlights trained on the SEAL all night? It would make his task considerably more difficult. If only . . .

The headlights flicked off.

Blade reacted instantly, silently unlocking the door on the park side and rolling onto the ground. He reached up and quietly closed the door, depressing the latch, insuring the SEAL was locked this time.

He would have just seconds to attain the cover of the park, the seconds it would require for any of the Watchers looking at the SEAL when the headlights went out to adjust to the abrupt darkness around the transport.

Move!

Blade ran, his body hunched over, making for the nearest vegetation. One thing bothered him, though. What had made that terrific roar he heard earlier? A mutate? What if he blundered across it in the gloom of night?

Ten yards remained.

If he reached the trees, he would search for any hidden Watchers and slit their throats, reduce the odds before morning.

Five yards.

Almost there! Thank the Spirit!

The bushes to his left parted, and a tall Watcher,

his M-16 cradled in his arms, stepped from concealment. "I tell you," he whispered to someone else,
"I think I saw something near it right after the
captain killed the lights."

"Get back in here!" the other person hissed.

"I need to be sure," the Watcher countered,
taking a step. "I can't see clearly from in . . ." He
stopped, his senses registering another presence.
He began to bring the M-16 around.

Blade spun and let loose with the Commando.
The heavy bullets caught the Watcher in the chest
and lifted him off of his feet, sending him
sprawling in a mangled heap.

Damn!

Just what he needed!

Blade sprinted the few yards to the trees and
dove into the undergrowth. Gunfire crackled from
different directions, snapping nearby branches and
twigs and striking several trees.

Blade stayed prone, waiting for the firing to
cease.

Doubledamn!

A Watcher, the companion of the one he shot,
came into view, his M-16 on automatic, deliberately spraying the area, meticulously moving the
rifle from left to right, covering every inch.

Stupid move!

Blade twisted and fired, ripping the Watcher
from his crotch to his brain, flinging him against a
tree.

Move! Move! Move!

Blade scrambled forward, knowing most of the
Watchers would converge on this spot. He plowed
under an overhanging plant and paused.

Which way?

Did it matter?

Yes.

He turned to the left, making for the parked

jeeps and the truck. If the Watchers concentrated on the spot he just left, they might leave their vehicles unattended.

The soil was loose under his elbows and knees, dampening any noise he made. The air near the ground was cool, refreshing his sweaty brow.

A single shot sounded from the direction of the building his friends were in.

Hickok's Henry.

Blade grinned. Hickok wouldn't shoot unless he had a target. In all the years Blade had known him, Hickok had never missed. So there were five less Watchers to contend with.

This is almost too easy, Blade told himself.

The Watchers, apparently angered at Hickok's shot, opened up on the building with a deafening crescendo of gunfire.

Good. There was no way they could hear him now.

Blade rose to a crouch and hurried toward the parked jeeps and the truck. He wanted to ascertain the contents of the truck. If the jeeps were unguarded, should he sabotage them? No. The Family would be able to use them after this was over.

Who was he kidding?

The Family would only get to use them if he and the others survived this fight.

Which was problematic at this point.

Blade reached the final fringe of vegetation and paused to reconnoiter. He could see the jeeps and the larger truck, parked in a row, their front ends all pointing at the Watchers' former headquarters in Thief River Falls.

There was no one in sight.

Perfect!

Blade rose, about to step from cover, when he detected motion to his right. He quickly dropped, lying flat, holding his breath.

Someone was near the vehicles, coming his way.

Blade spotted three figures walking past the jeeps. One of them was obviously a Watcher, but what in the world were the other two? They were huge, towering over the Watcher like adults over their children. Something about the manner in which they moved stirred Blade's mind. They were oddly familiar.

The trio came abreast of his hidden position.

Dear Spirit!

It couldn't be!

But it was.

In the center was a Watcher, in full iniform. He held a leash in each hand. And at the end of the leashes, one on either side of the Watcher, ambled two of the savage brutes, a male and a female.

It just couldn't be!

Blade closed his eyes, doubting his vision. The brutes were in league with the Watchers, serving as some sort of pet? Impossible! Simply impossible!

The Watchers were still firing on the building.

Blade opened his bewildered eyes.

The bizarre trio had stopped directly in front of him. The Watcher was observing the gunfire, the brutes standing mutely at his side.

What was going on here? Were the two brutes they killed, the male Geronimo slew and the female Joshua shot, a pair? Were they in Thief River Falls because they were with the group of Watchers headed by Joe? Were the brutes utilized as guard beasts? Blade absently shook his head, confused.

His hair brushed a leaf.

Instantly, the male brute stiffened and spun, growling, its beady eyes probing the foliage.

Damn!

Blade froze.

"What is it?" the Watcher asked the male brute. "What do you see, Krill?"

Krill? Blade's mind spun. The brutes had names?

Krill was sniffing loudly, attempting to detect a scent.

"What about you, Arla?" The Watcher faced the female. "Is there something out there?"

The female seemed uncertain, fidgeting on her leash.

Krill had calmed. He stood with his shoulders hunched and his head lowered.

"Guess not," the Watcher commented. "Heel." He began to turn, to take the brutes back the way they had come.

Maybe the brutes are kept in the rear of the truck, Blade silently speculated. This development added an entirely new dimension to the Watchers. Maybe he should return to the building and warn . . .

Blade's nose began tingling.

No!

Not now!

Before he could even try to control the impulse, he involuntarily sneezed.

Terrific!

Blade leaped to his feet, the Commando coming to bear, the stock pressed against his right hip. He fired, even as the two brutes jumped aside, their momentum wresting their leashes from the startled Watcher.

The Watcher was struck in the chest, his body jerking backward and colliding with one of the jeeps.

The brutes plunged into the park, one on either side of Blade.

Just great!

Blade ran into the street and whirled, covering the vegetation, his nerves taut.

Where were they?

What were they up to?

In the silence, he realized the firing on the building had ceased. When? Were his shots heard?

An M-16 abruptly chattered, the slugs biting into the ground at Blade's feet.

Blade turned and ran, keeping close to the vehicles for cover. He passed the fourth jeep and reached the truck.

"This way!" a voice behind him shouted. "The one from the van is over here!"

Big mouth.

Blade paused and peered into the back of the truck. The front half was piled high with boxes. The rest was littered with straw and reeked of a musky animal smell.

"Quick!" a Watcher yelled. "This way!"

Blade popped out from behind the truck. A solitary Watcher was running toward him. He raised the Commando, sighted, and blasted the Watcher from shoulder to shoulder.

In the park, one of the brutes roared.

Blade jogged away from the vehicles. His best bet would be to find a house he could hole up in until morning.

"After him!"

"This way!"

"He got Tim and Clyde!"

Blade heard more voices being raised as he reached the end of the park. The street he was on continued into a residential area. Good. With the park behind him, so were the brutes.

The guttural growl warned him of his error a split second before hairy arms encircled his waist and wrenched him into the air.

Blade instinctively surged against the constricting arms.

The brute snarled.

Blade dropped the Commando, realizing it was useless unless he could break free. He had to! If he didn't extricate himself before the Watchers caught up with him, he was as good as dead.

If he wasn't already.

Fangs suddenly sank into his right shoulder, and he arched his back, suppressing a scream, as acute pain tore through his brain.

No!

The brute was applying pressure to his waist, determined to crush the life from him.

Focus, he told himself! Focus! The Vegas were out of reach. He lacked the leverage to use his Bowies. His forearms, though, were loose. He reached across with his right hand and grabbed the dagger strapped to his left wrist, the hilt comforting in his grip as he swung his right forearm out and drove the point of the keen blade back and around his right hip. He felt the blade make contact, driving deep into vulnerable flesh.

The brute shrieked and released Blade.

Blade tumbled to the pavement, scraping his elbow, and landed on his back. He twisted, facing the brute.

It was Arla.

The dagger was imbedded in her lower abdomen, immediately above the buckskin loincloth she wore.

"Bring the flashlight!" a Watcher ordered, perhaps thirty yards distant.

Blade knew he had to act, and act now.

Arla was doubled over, her fingers spread over her stomach. She looked at Blade and hissed, straightening and lunging for him, her teeth bared.

Blade drew the Vegas in a cross draw, pointed the pistols at the brute's face, and fired at point-blank range, first the right Vega, then the left, two, three, four shots, directly into her head.

Arla rocked on her heels, her massive body swaying as she tried to focus her fading sentience.

Fall, damn you!

Blade shot her two more times.

The brute collapsed, sagging to its knees, then toppling over, sprawled in the street.

Blade holstered his Vegas, retrieved the Commando, and rose. His right shoulder was throbbing, and he could feel his blood oozing down his chest and back. He shuffled off, passing several decayed structures. At an intersection, he bore right.

The sounds of pursuit had faded.

A white frame house, or the remains of one, attracted his attention to his left.

Blade crossed a weed-choked yard and cautiously entered the house through the front doorway. A door was on the ground next to the entrance. He sagged against a wall and caught his breath.

Outside, footsteps pounded in the street. A light appeared, bobbing as the Watcher carrying the flashlight ran.

There were four of them. They stopped ten yards from the house.

"Which way did he go?" one of them asked.

"No way to tell," another replied.

"Did you see what the bastard did to Arla?" questioned still another.

"Arla, hell!" exploded the first one. "Who cares about her? The prick just wasted four of *us!*"

"I know who cares what happened to Arla," said the fourth man. "Krill. The captain has him leashed, but he's hard to control. He'll tear this sucker to shreds for what he did to Arla."

"This guy could have gone in any direction," commented the first Watcher. "Let's leave him to Krill. We've got to secure the perimeter on the ones inside."

The Watchers departed, walking slowly.

Blade stuck his head out the doorway, listening. He could barely distinguish their conversation.

"When did the captain say the reinforcements will arrive?" one of them was asking. "And how many are coming?"

"Forty troops," answered another. "Tomorrow, about six in the evening. These yokels don't stand a chance!"

"Tell that to Arla and our seven dead mates."

"We'll teach them! No one messes with First Company. No one!"

First Company? Reinforcements on the way? They must have a radio with them. Damn! Blade leaned his head against the wall and closed his weary eyes. His right side and his right shoulder were tormenting him with piercing, burning pain. Dear Spirit, how they hurt!

So what should he do now?

Blade opened his eyes and stepped to the doorway. Should he try to return to Hickok and the others while it was still dark? Or should he wait until morning? What was the wisest course of action?

The matter was abruptly taken from his hands.

A huge, fluid, ebony shape drifted across the intersection.

Krill!

On his trail so soon?

Blade ran from the house and turned left, keeping to the middle of the street. Staying in the house would be suicide. Krill would have him boxed in, ripe for the kill.

In the open, at least, he had a slim chance.

Very slim.

With his ears tuned for the patter of feet behind him, Blade ran further into the stygian wasteland of Thief River Falls.

14

"It's been so quiet for so long," Joshua commented.

"I know," Bertha agreed. They were lying on the floor by the front door, Bertha with her eyes at the jamb, alert for any indication of movement.

"What do you think they're up to?" Joshua asked.

"I wish I knew," Bertha replied. "I don't like this sittin' and waitin' for something to happen. I'm the type that likes to make things happen."

"Like Hickok," Joshua noted.

"Like White Meat." Bertha grinned. She glanced at the stairway. "Where the hell is he anyway?"

"He must have fired the shot from the roof earlier," Joshua speculated.

"He'd pull a stunt like that, for sure," Bertha remarked proudly.

"I thought the Watchers would never stop firing at us," Joshua mentioned. "There's a high probability Hickok struck one of them."

"You can bet your butt I hit one," Hickok

stated, coming down the stairs. "I always hit my
targets."

"Did you kill him?" Bertha inquired hopefully.

"Need you ask?" Hickok responded in a mock-
hurt tone.

Bertha giggled. "You sure are somethin' else,
white boy."

Hickok joined them on the floor. He peeked
around the door. "Any sign?" he asked.

"Not a thing," Bertha answered. "They've been
quiet ever since the shooting earlier."

"Did you hear the Commando?" Hickok questioned.

"How can you tell the difference?" Joshua
wanted to know.

"I heard it," Bertha nodded. "I hope he's all
right. He should of stayed in the SEAL."

"Blade knows what he's doing," Hickok said
confidently.

"I just hope his ass is still alive," Bertha
retorted.

"Should we go out and see?" Joshua looked at
Hickok.

"Are you nuts, pard?" Hickok demanded.

"I beg your pardon?" Joshua responded.

"You take one step out this door," Hickok told
Joshua, "and the Watchers will perforate you."

"So we do not even attempt to assist Blade?"
Joshua asked.

"We do not."

"I don't think . . ." Joshua began.

"Who asked you?" Hickok snapped. "Who's the
Warrior here, me or you? I'm telling you Blade is
on his own. He knows it. He's a big boy. Like I just
told Bertha, Blade knows what he's doing."

"I wasn't striving to usurp your authority,"
Joshua explained.

"I understand, Josh," Hickok informed him.

"Listen. I'm a little tired, and a little sore, and now a little cranky. We all could use some rest. Why don't you nap for a spell?"

"Are you certain it's safe?" Joshua inquired.

"I don't think the Watchers will try anything until morning," Hickok opined. "It'll be safe. We'll wake you in a while."

"I don't know if I could sleep," Joshua observed.

"Try."

Joshua moved to the blankets and reclined on the mattress.

"You were a bit hard on him, weren't you?" Bertha whispered.

"Guess I get a mite irritable when my head feels like a horse is stomping on my brain," Hickok said.

"Why don't you get some sleep?" Bertha asked. "I can watch the door."

"Wish I could," Hickok stated.

"You got somethin' more important to do?" Bertha quizzed him.

"Sure do." Hickok glanced around the room.

"Like what?" Bertha demanded.

"I'm searching this place high and low," Hickok said. "Somewhere in this building is a hidden transmitter, and I intend to find it."

"What good will it do you?" Bertha questioned.

"If I can figure out how to work it," Hickok replied, "I can listen in on the Watchers. Would give us an edge."

"You figure they have an transmitter with them?" Bertha inquired.

"I reckon," Hickok responded, rising. "It makes sense. They would want to keep in touch with one another. You said they're scattered in differrent towns, all over the place?"

"Yep," Bertha confirmed.

"So they must have a system of keeping in touch," Hickok speculated. "A system they'd like to hide from everybody else."

"You want me to help you?" Bertha asked.

"Nope. You stay at the door. I'll relieve you later."

"Good luck, White Meat," Bertha encouraged him.

"Thanks. I'll need it." Hickok walked to the bar, debating where to begin his search. The transmitter Harry and Pete mentioned was in this building, but it could take forever finding it, and he didn't have that much time. He placed the Henry on top of the bar.

What the blazes would a transmitter look like?

Hickok leaned against the bar, reflecting. The Family owned several portable radios, actually small transmitters, utilized during and immediately after the Big Blast. They were stored in the rear of the armory, gathering dust over the decades. Would the one he was looking for resemble the old Family equipment? Or had they altered the design in the intervening century? And how would the thing be powered? Electricity from the generator? Batteries? Or the innovative solar chips developed prior to the Third World War?

Hickok looked down at Joshua, asleep on the mattress. He felt sorry for the trauma Joshua was experiencing, and wondered how Josh would hold up in the morning, when the Watchers were certain to launch a full-scale assault. "Never should have brought you along, pard," he muttered under his breath.

Joshua's mattress was positioned against the bar, and as Hickok's eyes roved over the wooden front panels near Joshua's head, an idea struck him.

Why not?

Hickok moved around the bar and studied it closely. Under the counter top were two rows of shelves, each shelf filled with various bottles of liquor. Under the shelves, the center section of the bar was empty, consisting of a wooden panel. To the right and the left, though, were cabinets with closed doors. The stereo was in the lower right cabinet, as he'd discovered earlier.

Hickok knelt and opened the right cabinet, double-checking.

Nothing but the stereo, some glasses, and metal trays.

He stepped to the second cabinet and opened the door.

This time he found forks, spoons, knives, and plastic plates and cups.

So much for his brainstorm!

Hickok rested his elbows on the counter and sighed.

Where to look next? Downstairs? Or upstairs? There was nowhere else in this room the transmitter could be hidden, unless it was recessed into one of the walls. Maybe he . . .

Whoa!

Hickok straightened and stared at the back of the bar again. Very odd. The two cabinets extended a good two and a half feet from the front of the bar, allowing ample space for whatever was being stored inside. Made sense. But the middle of the bar also extended the same distance, and that definitely did not make sense. The person behind the bar would be constantly cracking his knees on the center wooden panel. Wouldn't it be smarter to have the middle of the bar recessed?

Of course it would!

Hickok crouched and tapped the knuckles of his right hand against the center panel. It sounded hollow, but that might not mean a thing. There was only one way to be positive.

Hickok ran his fingers around the edges of the

panel. If his assumption was correct, there should be a hidden latch or a knob or . . . grooves. There was a narrow groove on each side of the panel. He pressed his fingers into the grooves and lifted.

The panel slid up and out.

Hickok leaned the panel against the right cabinet and smiled. What was the name of that dude he'd read about years ago? Sherlock Holmes, wasn't it? Well, Mr. Sherlock Holmes, eat your heart out!

The portable transmitter was green, about a foot square, and covered with switches, dials, and several meters.

"Got ya!" Hickok elated.

"Did you find it?" Bertha called from the door.

"Of course," Hickok replied. He lifted the transmitter and carefully placed it on the counter.

"Can I come see?" Bertha asked eagerly.

"Stay by that door," Hickok directed.

Joshua slowly stood, stretching. "Is it my turn to pull guard duty?" he inquired, yawning. His eyes fell on the trasmitter and widened. "What have you got there?"

"A transmitter." Hickok peered at the white lettering below each switch and dial. "If I only knew how to work this blasted thing!"

Joshua came around the bar. "Let me have a look."

"You know how to operate one of these?" Hickok asked.

"Although the ones we have at the Home no longer function," Joshua explained, "my curiosity was aroused when I saw them for the first time. I distinctly recall reading the instruction sheets and wishing they were still operational. My memory isn't perfect, but . . ." He tried reading the labels. "If we only had some light in here."

"Want me to turn on the lights?" Bertha offered.

"No way," Hickok retorted. "The Watchers might decide to take some potshots at us."

"I know!" Joshua abruptly exclaimed. He returned to the front of the bar, bent over, and stood, holding his pouch aloft. "I think I have them in here."

"What?" Hickok asked.

"You'll see," Joshua said excitedly. "I know I put them in here after I used them to heat Bertha's can of food."

"What?" Hickok repeated.

"These." Joshua opened his left palm, revealing the box of matches taken from the motorcyclist.

"Way to go, pard!" Hickok grinned.

Joshua rejoined Hickok, opened the box, and ignited one of the all-purpose matches by striking it against the counter top. He held the match up and squinted at the transmitter, reading the labels aloud. "Modulation. Charging. Transmit Mode. Receive Mode. Here it is!" he happily declared. "Power." He flicked a toggle switch and the unit suddenly hummed. One of the meters above the power switch lit up, illuminating a small scale. A thin black needle hovered at the left side of the needle.

"What we want to do," Hickok informed Joshua, "is listen in on the Watchers without them being any the wiser. Can we do it?"

"Easily," Joshua replied. "This should do it." He flicked another switch, this one marked Receive Mode.

Abrupt crackling and static emanated from a speaker in the upper right of the unit.

"There's nothing there," Hickok commented, disappointed.

"Possibly they are not broadcasting," Joshua reasoned. "Or we could be on the wrong frequency."

"Doubt it," Hickok disagreed. "They would have this gizmo set for their frequency, all right. Who else would they listen to?"

"Then all we can do is wait," Joshua stated.

"And you know how Hickok is at waiting," Bertha chuckled.

"If patience was gold," Joshua remarked, "Hickok would be the poorest man alive."

Bertha laughed. "Hey, that's pretty good, Josh! You're learning!"

Hickok shook his head. "Just great! It isn't bad enough I have Geronimo on my case all the time, but now I'll have to put up with you too?"

Joshua grinned.

"First you blow away a brute," Hickok stated, "and now you're telling jokes. You're changing, pard."

Joshua's expression altered, a cloud seeming to cross his face. "I certainly am, aren't I?" he stated wistfully.

"So what's our next move?" Bertha inquired, hastily attempting to change the subject.

"Like Josh said," Hickok answered sighing, "there's nothing we can do but wait. The next move is theirs."

Joshua, deep in thought, noticed the match was extinguished. He dropped it to the floor, wondering if, come morning, their lives would be snuffed out as easily as the flame from the match.

"We haven't heard anything in a while," Bertha mentioned. "I hope Blade is all right."

"I told you not to worry about him," Hickok said. "If I know Blade, he's relaxing right now, working on a plan to get us out of this mess."

"Relaxing?" Bertha repeated doubtfully.

"Sure. He's probably hiding in the park somewhere, or in one of the nearby houses, taking it easy, waiting for the right moment to strike. Blade isn't the kind to sweat the small stuff."

"You call this mess we're in small stuff?" Bertha asked.

"It's no big deal." Hickok shrugged.

"You're crazy, White Meat," Bertha stated. "If you think this is small stuff, I'd hate to see what you'd call big trouble."

15

I'm in big trouble here, Blade mentally told himself as he jogged along the darkened streets of Thief River Falls. He'd run over four miles at least, always staying within the town limits, crisscrossing and zigzagging, first one street for a few blocks, then, at random, another avenue for several more blocks, but never for any great distance in a straight line. He wouldn't give Krill the advantage of predicting his direction, of being able to race ahead and ambush him.

So far, so good. It appeared to be working. But combined with his injuries, the strain was taking a severe toll.

Blade's breathing was becoming labored, and an excruciating pang periodically seared his right side. The pain in his shoulder was a constant, agonizing presence. He required rest, but could he afford to stop? There had been no sign of Krill since the intersection. Had the brute abandoned the chase? Why would it hang back so long? If it was simply an unthinking animal, craving revenge for Arla, surely it would have attacked by now?

He had to rest!

Blade paused, listening. The wind was increasing, rustling the leaves on a stand of trees to his right. An owl hooted. The night seemed perfectly normal.

Ahead, maybe fifteen yards away, was a brick house, one of the few with a front door still intact.

Blade ran to the door and stopped, scaning for any indication Krill was in the area.

Nothing.

Another spasm rocked his body. What was going on? Was one of his ribs broken? Arla had gripped him around the waist, though, not his chest. Was there internal damage from the bullet or Arla's crushing grasp? Whatever, he felt a compelling need to lie down.

Blade gingerly opened the door and entered the house, closing the door behind him. The air was stale and musty. He successfully resisted another impulse to sneeze.

Two doors opened into the room he was in, a former living room containing dust-covered furniture and furnishings. Both doors were ajar. He walked to the front door and pushed it open, revealing a bedroom. The second door was to the kitchen. Neither displayed any evidence of recent habitation. The window in the bedroom was gone, but a small window in the kitchen was intact and closed. He shut both doors and moved to the sofa. Tiny particles of dust rose into the air as he sat down and rested his head on the back of the creaking sofa.

Now, if Krill tried to attack, the brute would need to come through one of the three doors. It wouldn't be much of a warning, but it would give him a few precious moments to bring the Commando to bear.

Blade closed his tired eyes, his thoughts drifting. What was his beloved Jenny doing? Was she moping, pining for his safe return? How he wished he could be with her, holding her in his arms, listening to her tender words of affection!

What was that?

Blade snapped to attention. He was positive he'd heard a scraping noise. Was it Krill? He waited and waited, but the house was filled with soothing quiet, with a comforting sense of solitude.

Must be my nerves, he reflected.

Blade leaned back and closed his eyes again. Memories of his parents flooded his mind. His mother he'd never known; she had died giving birth to him. His father had served as Family Leader until four years ago, when he was killed by a mutate. Blade relived the incident again. His father was on a hunting expedition with two other men. They fell behind, while one of them removed a stone from his boot. Without warning, a mutate, a former mountain lion, charged from the brush and ripped his father to shreds. The mutate vanished into the woods, leaving a torn and bloody body and a profound mystery in its wake.

Mutates! How he hated them! What could possibly transform your average puma into a hairless horror, covered with large blistering sores, oozing pus everywhere, its skin split and shriveled? Mutates were insatiably ravenous, devouring anything and everything they saw, even other mutates.

Everyone knew that fact.

And yet . . .

The mutate responsible for his father's demise did not devour the body. It did not even try to. Nor did it go after the other two Family men.

Odd.

Even odder was the story the two men had told. They had claimed this particular mutate wore a wide leather collar. Imagine! Although they were

respected members of the Family, no one had
really believed they had actually seen a collar.

Blade missed his father. Plato had assumed
leadership of the Family after his father's death,
and he knew Plato expected him to become Leader
some day. He recalled the pressures and problems
his father was forced to face daily, and he sincerely
doubted he wanted any part of it. Let someone else
be Leader. He would devote himself to raising a
family of his own, to enjoying a peaceful existence,
married to Jenny, living in one of the cabins
reserved for the couples. He'd relinquish his
Warrior rank and . . .

Something scratched nearby.

Blade, fatigued, slowly opened his eyes, then
froze, involuntarily gawking.

Krill was standing in the bedroom doorway, a
hulking monstrosity with his massive body tensed
for a leap.

How the . . .?

Move! Blade's mind screamed at him, and he
swept the Commando up even as Krill jumped,
firing, the slugs ripping into Krill's thick torso,
slowing the brute's momentum, enabling Blade to
roll aside and fall to the floor as Krill crashed onto
the sofa.

Damn!

Blade pressed the tigger as Krill lunged at him,
the brute's left arm connecting with the
Commando barrel and sending it flying from
Blade's desperate hands.

Krill snarled and grabbed for Blade's legs.

Blade rolled to his left and swiftly rose to his
feet, drawing the Vegas, as Krill stood and came
toward him, hissing and growling. Come and get it,
sucker! He aimed the automatics at the brute's
furious face, intent on doing to Krill exactly as he
had done to Arla.

Fate, however, had other plans.

Blade too two steps backward, wanting to be sure of his aim, his entire attention concentrated on Krill. His feet collided with something hard and, startled, he glanced down, too late, as he tripped over a wooden chair and tumbled to the foor.

Krill roared and closed in.

Before Blade could regain his balance, Krill stood over him and grabbed his wrists. Blade vainly struggled to free his arms as the brute applied pressure, twisting his wrists and squeezing, forcing his wrists to bend at an unnatural angle.

Krill's pointed fangs were exposed as the brute grinned at its enemy.

Blade had no other choice. He was forced to drop the Vegas.

Krill released Blade's wrists and straightened, glaring, confident of impending victory.

I'm not finished yet, bastard! Blade drew his knees up to his chest and drove his legs upward, slamming his feet into the brute's crotch.

He connected.

Krill shrieked and gurgled, almost falling, his huge hands cupping his groin area as he staggered away from Blade. The brute stumbled against the sofa and stopped, whining.

Blade heaved erect, whipping his Bowies out, and charged. He must act now, before Krill recovered!

Krill attempted to sidestep, unsuccessfully.

Blade barreled into the brute, bowling him over, and both of them fell onto the sofa.

Krill swung his right fist at Blade's head.

Blade ducked, raised his right Bowie, and bured it to the hilt in Krill's brawny chest.

Krill surged upward, roaring, enraged, trying to dislodge the man pinning him down.

Blade swept the left Bowie up, tensed, and plunged the blade into Krill's body within an inch of his other knife.

Krill's arms flapped wildly, his left catching Blade a glancing blow on the side of his head and knocking him onto the floor.

Blade rose, reaching for one of the Solingen throwing knives strapped to the small of his back. He'd lost one in the rat he'd killed in Bertha's room. That left him with two throwing knives. One of his daggers was imbedded in Arla's gut, leaving him with his last dagger, tied to his right calf.

Krill was motionless.

Was the brute faking?

Blade cautiously moved closer.

Krill's eyes were closed, his body immobile. Blood was pouring from the bullet wounds inflicted by the Commando, and oozing around the Bowie knives, still protruding from the brute's chest.

The damn thing was finally dead!

Blade sighed in relief and sat on the arm of the sofa, absently gazing at his fallen foe. Where did the brutes come from? How were the Watchers able to control them? A simple leash couldn't be . . .

He stopped, staring.

In the heat of their conflict, he had never noticed Krill was still wearing the leash. It was draped over his left shoulder and dangled down his broad back. Krill, Blade surmised, must have broken loose from the Watchers, wanting revenge for Arla. So! The Watchers did not exercise complete domination over their savage charges.

What should he do now? Return to Hickok, Geronimo, and the others and warn them reinforcements were coming?

Blade's eyes drifted across Krill's neck as he

began to rise, then suddenly he stiffened and leaned forward, peering closely at the brute.

It couldn't be!

Dear Spirit! No!

But it was.

The leash was attached to Krill's neck, affixed to a . . . wide . . . leather . . . collar!

Blade, stunned, his mind spinning, sat up, pondering the incredible implications.

Was it possible? Was the story true after all? The mutate responsible for his father's death reportedly wore a leather collar. Was there a connection between the Watchers and . . .

Blade abruptly realized Krill's eyes were open, staring at him, gleaming with feral intensity. He tried to bring one of the Solingen knives into play, his reaction sluggish.

Krill snarled, bringing both of his granite fists sweeping in, crashing them against Blade's head, boxing him on the ears.

Blade endeavored to rise, but his eyes rolled and he slipped from the sofa and landed prone on the floor.

The brute stood. It roared and gazed at Blade, licking its thick lips.

Krill bent over the prostrate Warrior.

16

Joshua was pulling guard duty at the door. Hickok and Bertha were resting near the bar. Morning was still an hour away, but already some of the early birds were chirping their optimistic greeting to a new day.

Something was going on near the park.

Joshua could see a flurry of activity at the edge of the park, but he couldn't quite make out what they were up to. He turned toward the sleeping duo.

"Hickok!" Joshua called.

The gunman was instantly awake, his senses fully alert. He crossed the room and crouched next to Joshua. "What's up?"

"The Watchers are engaged in a bustle of movement," Joshua replied. "Their motivation and intention are not readily apparent."

"When's your birthday?" Hickok unexpectedly inquired.

"What's that have to do with anything?" Joshua demanded, surprised at the query.

"Oh, nothing much." Hickok grinned. "Just

thought I'd get you a dictionary from the library for your birthday. Your vocabulary is pitiful."

"I do evince a certain propensity for rather grandiose forms of expression at times," Joshua seriously admitted.

Hickok playfully slapped Joshua on the back. "You're all right, pard. Let me have a look-see."

"Is somethin' up?" Bertha asked sleepily, joining them.

"Don't know yet," Hickok responded. He peered outside. The Watchers were hastily doing . . . something . . . near the park.

"Did you hear anything on that radio?" Bertha questioned Joshua.

Joshua shook his head. "Just static. They haven't made a call all night."

"Bertha," Hickok directed. "Go up on the roof. Wake up that lazy Injun if he's asleep and see if you can tell what the Watchers are up to."

"I can do it," Joshua interjected. "Bertha's arm shouldn't . . ."

"Don't you worry none," Bertha interrupted. "I ain't no invalid. Be back in a jiffy." She left them.

"What do you think they're doing?" Joshua asked Hickok.

The Warrior shrugged. "Who knows? We'll find out soon enough. You can bet . . ."

The Watchers' transmiter unit began sputtering and crackling, followed by a raspy voice speaking in precise, clipped phrasing. "Charlie-Bravo-One-Three-Niner-Niner. This is Charlie-Lima-Two-Four-Seven-Seven. Do you copy? Over?"

Almost immediately, another man responded. "Roger, Charlie-Lima-Two-Four-Seven-Seven. We copy," he said acknowledging receipt of the transmission. "What is your ETA?"

"Still set at eighteen hundred," the first voice stated. "Has your status changed?"

"Negative. Containment still in effect. The captain would like to speak with Colonel Jarvis."

There was a protracted pause, and a gruff voice came on the line.

"Colonel Jarvis here. Williams, are you there?"

"Yes, sir," a younger-sounding officer replied. "This is Captain Williams."

"What can I do for you, Williams?" Colonel Jarvis asked.

"I would like permission to execute a plan I have," Williams said.

"What kind of plan?" Jarvis wanted to know.

"I believe I can force them to surrender, sir."

"Oh? First give me an update on the current situation," Jarvis ordered.

"Sir . . . ?" Captain Williams hesitated, apparently reluctant to report.

"Are you hard of hearing?" Colonel Jarvis demanded. "Provide me with an update. Now."

"An unknown number are still contained within our building," Williams responded.

"Any idea yet what happened to our boys stationed there?" Jarvis inquired.

"No idea, sir."

"Any losses on your end?" Jarvis inquired.

Dead silence.

"Captain Williams," Jarvis stated harshly, "you're starting to piss me off. And you know what I can do to officers who piss me off."

"Yes, sir," Williams quickly answered.

"Then report."

"One of their Warriors broke containment," Williams stated.

Joshua gripped Hickok's right arm. "How do they know Blade is a Warrior?"

"Hush!" Hickok snapped. "Listen!"

"You neutralized the Warrior, of course," Colonel Jarvis was saying.

"Negative, sir."

"What?" Jarvis sounded annoyed. "He . . . I take it this Warrior is a man?"

"Yes, sir."

"Is he still at large?"

"Negative, sir. We have him in our custody," Williams said.

Joshua took a step toward the radio. "They've got Blade!"

"You still haven't told me if you sustained any casualties," Jarvis reminded Williams.

"Yes, sir. We did, sir." Captain Williams hedged.

"Williams," Colonel Jarvis warned, "you better tell me the body count, and you better do it now, or when I get there you'll be sorry you were ever born."

"We lost . . ." Captain Williams couldn't seem to bring himself to say it. "The body count is eight, sir," he finally blurted.

"*You've lost eight men?*" Colonel Jarvis exploded.

"No, sir," Williams meekly replied.

"No?"

"Seven men, sir," Williams reported, "and one of our Rovers. Arla, the female."

"*One of the Rovers?*" Colonel Jarvis practically screamed.

"Yes, sir."

"Do you know how costly they are to produce?" Jarvis asked.

"Yes, sir," Williams replied.

Colonel Jarvis sighed. "Very well. Any sign of the other couple assigned to Thief River Falls?"

"Negative, sir."

"Is the male . . . what was his name?" Jarvis inquired.

"Krill, sir. He's badly injured. We have him in the back of the truck. Our medic doesn't think he'll last out the hour. He captured the Warrior, sir," Williams elaborated.

"Damn!" Colonel Jarvis was furious. "This Warrior must be one mean son of a bitch!"

"No argument here, sir," Williams said.

"So what is your plan?"

"I request permission to use the prisoner as bait. We will give the ones inside an ultimatum. Either they surrender, or we will kill the one we have. Do I have your permission?" Captain Williams asked hopefully.

"Permission granted," Colonel Jarvis agreed. "But Williams . . ."

"Yes, sir?"

"You have a dozen men left, right?"

"Yes, sir."

"Under no circumstances," Colonel Jarvis directed, "are you to engage them unless as a defensive maneuver. Understood?"

"Yes, sir," Williams stated.

"Hold them until we arrive and we'll mop them up," Jarvis predicted.

"No problem," Williams promised.

"Captain . . ." Jarvis added as an afterthought.

"Yes, Colonel Jarvis?"

"Don't feel too bad," Jarvis suggested. "You know the reputation these Warriors have."

"I certainly do."

"Any identity on the prisoner?" Jarvis asked.

"He won't talk," Williams replied. "But from the file description I'd guess it's Blade."

"Blade?" Colonel Jarvis sounded impressed. "Then Hickok and Geronimo must be inside."

"That's my assessment," Williams concurred.

"You heard what they did to the Trolls?" Colonel Jarvis inquired.

"It was in the classified pouch I received about two weeks ago," Captain Williams stated.

"Then you know how dangerous they are. Don't take chances. Sit on them until I arrive."

"Will do, sir."

"Charlie-Lima-Two-Four-Seven-Seven, over and out."

The compact radio buzzed with static.

"I don't understand," Joshua said.

"That makes two of us," Hickok conceded.

"They knew about your fight with the Trolls!" Joshua stated. "How?"

"Forget the Trolls!" Hickok rejoined. "They know all about us, all about Alpha Triad. For that matter, they seem to know all about the Family and the Home."

"How?" Joshua repeated.

"I wish to blazes I knew," Hickok said. "None of this makes any sense!"

"Didn't Blade believe there was a connection between the Trolls and the Watchers?" Joshua asked.

"Yeah. But he had no idea what kind of connection."

"How would they know about the Family?" Joshua questioned.

"Josh," Hickok said, peeved, "you ask too many questions. I'm just as much in the dark as you are. Right now, it doesn't really matter how they know about us. We have something more important to worry about."

"We do?"

"They've got Blade, remember?" Hickok growled.

"What are we going to do?" Joshua inquired.

"Go up on the roof," Hickok instructed him, "and get Geronimo and Bertha. We need a conference."

"On my way." Joshua ran up the stairs.

What *were* they going to do? Hickok leaned

against the wall, debating their course of action. The first priority, obviously, was to free Blade from the clutches of the Watchers. But how? He glanced out the door, noting the activity near the park had ceased. They sky was still too dark to distinguish details accurately, but there was . . . something . . . or . . . someone . . . near the line of trees.

Hickok walked to the bar and retrieved his Henry from the counter top. Captain Williams had mentioned an ultimatum, one the Watchers would undoubtedly present at daybreak or shortly thereafter, which didn't leave much time to devise a plan to rescue Blade. The Watchers still were a dozen soldiers strong, exactly three times the number of guns Hickok could rely on. A considerable advantage.

There was a commotion upstairs, and Geronimo, Bertha, and Joshua appeared.

"What's this about the Watchers?" Geronimo asked as he descended the stairs. "Joshua says they know all about us?"

"Evidently," Hickok confirmed. He proceeded to narrate the monitored conversation between Captain Williams and Colonel Jarvis.

"So what's our next move?" Geronimo questioned when Hickok concluded his explanation.

"I'm open to any suggestions," Hickok stated.

"*Inside the building! Listen up!*" abruptly boomed a voice from outside.

"What the . . ." Hickok began. He hurried to the door, the rest on his heels.

"*I know you can hear me!*" shouted the voice.

"How can he make his words so loud?" Bertha inquired, puzzled.

"He's utilizing a device designated a bull horn," Joshua conjectured. "The Family owns a pair, inoperative because we lack the batteries required for proper performance."

"I'm definitely getting you that dictionary for your birthday," Hickok muttered.

"*I know you can hear me!*" the voice reiterated.

"Can anyone see who's talkin'?" Bertha asked.

"No," Geronimo answered. "He's probably in the park."

"*My name is Captain Williams.*" Williams spoke slowly, deliberately, enunciating each word.

"I thought I recognized the creep," Hickok said.

"*Pay attention to what I am about to say . . .*"

"What's that?" Geronimo leaned forward, spotting the result of the Watchers' earlier labors. As dawn approached, the light was rapidly increasing. "It's Blade!" he exclaimed.

The others pressed closer to the opening.

"*As you can plainly see by now,*" Williams declared, "*we have your friend in custody.*"

"He's tied to a pole!" Bertha stated.

"*We have secured him to a pole. Any rescue attempt would be futile.*"

"He's not moving," Bertha said. "Are you sure he's still alive?"

"That's what they said on the radio," Hickok replied.

"*We will cut you to ribbons if you try to free him,*" Williams declared.

"I'd like to cut you to ribbons," Hickok said.

"*Listen closely! Sunrise will occur soon. You have until the sun is completely above the horizon to surrender, or we will shoot your friend.*"

"Doesn't give us much time," Geronimo commented.

"*Remember!*" Williams arrogantly bellowed. "*The second the sun is completely visible, we'll turn your friend into a sieve!*"

"Do we surrender?" Joshua inquired.

"Do rabbits fly?" Hickok responded.

"Then what do we do, White Meat?" Bertha frowned, concerned. "They have us right where they want us."

"Do they?" Hickok said, grinning.

"I've seen that look before," Geronimo noted. "It usually means your minuscule mind has come up with a plan."

"Do we have any rope in this place?" Hickok asked them.

"I haven't seen any," Geronimo answered. "How long do you need it to be?"

Hickok absently rubbed his chin as he calculated. "At least ten feet. You can drop the rest of the distance."

"We have the blankets," Bertha said. "If we tied them together and used some odds and ends, we could get ten feet. Why?"

Hickok began pacing. "The way I see it, we've got to make our move at sunrise, when they'll be expecting us to surrender." He faced Joshua. "Is the Ruger loaded?"

"Yes," Joshua replied.

"Give it to me," Hickok ordered. He took the revolver and slid the barrel under his belt, just to the right of the buckle, leaving the grips and the hammer free for quick action. "This will give me eighteen."

"Eighteen?" Bertha repeated.

"Yeah. Eighteen shots."

"What are you going to use them for?" Joshua inquired.

"I'll need them," Hickok smirked, "when I go out the front door. Now here's my plan . . ."

17

Jenny found him on a small knoll east of the cabins, sitting on a boulder, gazing at the spectacular colors emblazoning the eastern sky.

"Dawn is almost here," she stated the obvious.

"You couldn't sleep either," he asked her, his kindly blue eyes laced with a trace of sadness.

"I've been unable to sleep since he left," Jenny revealed.

"I too am experiencing difficulty with my repose," he said.

"Do you regret sending Alpha Triad out into the world, Plato?" she questioned him.

"Frankly, I'm torn both ways," he admitted. "You know I love Blade, and I'm fond of the others too. I do regret sending them on their mission. At the same time, I know the importance of their task. I know the Family will not survive unless they succeed."

"You did the right thing," she assured him.

"Thank you." He smiled. "It does my soul good to hear you say that. I need your support."

"You have it," Jenny assured him. She put her left hand on his right shoulder and gently squeezed. "All of us love you. We might disagree at times, but always remember you have our loyal and abiding support."

Plato rose, his knees wobbly, weaving as he stood. "I wish I could develop a cure for this damnable arthritis!"

"It's getting worse, isn't it?" Jenny inquired.

"Let's forget our cares and woes," Plato said, ignoring her query. He stretched, watching the sun begin to emerge above the horizon. "What do you say to visiting my cabin for breakfast? I'm sure Nadine will be delighted to have you visit."

"I don't want to impose," Jenny mentioned.

"Nonsense," Plato said, overruling her objection. "I'll inform my dear wife we spent all night out here under the stars. Let's see if we can make her jealous."

Jenny laughed. "You're as playful as ever!"

"At my age," Plato amended, "you're frisky, not playful."

They strolled toward the cabins, savoring the fresh morning air and the chirping of the birds.

"It's a beautiful morning," Jenny declared.

"And just think," Plato reassured her. "Wherever the Alpha Triad is at this very moment, they are undoubtedly enjoying this crisp new dawn as much as we are."

"You think so?"

"You don't believe me?"

"I don't know . . ." she began.

"Where's all this loyal and abiding support I'm supposed to receive?" Plato grinned.

"You know I trust you," Jenny said.

"Then stop worrying!" Plato advised her. "Relax. We'll have a big meal and gossip about everyone else. Did you hear the question one of the children asked yesterday in anatomy class?"

"You're terrible," Jenny chuckled. "I don't

know how Nadine puts up with you!"

"She thinks I'm a hunk." Plato smirked.

Jenny chuckled. "You are. And so is my Blade."

"Who, at this very second," Plato speculated, striving to ease her anxiety, "is alive and well and invariably thinking of you."

"I know he's still alive," Jenny affirmed. "I can feel it, deep down. But I'm troubled . . ."

"About what?" Plato cut her off. "You just said you feel he's alive, and you know he can handle himself competently."

"I guess you're right," she agreed. "I really shouldn't upset myself. After all, he's with Hickok and Geronimo. What could possibly beat all of them?"

18

The Watchers.

Through a pervading haze and numbing pain, Blade struggled to regain his concentration.

The Watchers. Where were they?

Blade dimly remembered being stripped of everything except for his pants. They had dug a hole at the fringe of the park, directly across from the building his friends occupied. The Watchers had placed a tall post in the hole, packed in the dirt, and tied their captive to the pole, securing his wrists and his ankles so tightly the circulation was constricted.

His head was pounding.

Blade recalled the shouting and dimly registered the message. He knew the consequences. According to their training, Warriors would never surrender, under any circumstances. Hickok and Geronimo would be forced to let the Watchers shoot him.

There wasn't much time left.

Where were the Watchers? Were any of them paying any attention to him, or were they all riveted on the building?

Did it matter?

Blade felt his full consciousness return, and he carefully opened his eyes. He could see the SEAL, and beyond the vehicle the Watchers' former headquarters. None of the Watchers, though. They were probably scattered around the area, in hiding, waiting for sunrise.

The bonds holding his wrists seemed slightly loose.

Blade cautiously flexed his steely muscles and felt the ropes give a fraction.

Good!

The sun was rising.

Blade surged against the ropes, attempting to minimize his body movements, hoping to prevent the Watchers from detecting his efforts. The Watchers would be intent on the front door of the building, waiting for those inside to surrender.

I can do it! Blade told himself. If he applied sufficient pressure, eventually the ropes would slacken enough to free his arms.

The only question was, could he succeed before the sun was completely above the horizon?

Several Watchers suddenly appeared on the buildings nearest the headquarters, their rifles pointing at the front door.

Sweat coated his powerful frame as Blade strained against his bonds, his body quivering.

Just a few more minutes! All he needed was a few measely minutes!

Someone was moving in the park behind him, rustling the underbrush.

Blade was on the verge of freeing his hands, and wondering what his next move should be, considering his legs were still fastened to the post, when the one thing he didn't expect to happen happened.

The front door opened and Hickok stepped outside, holding his arms over his head, grinning like an idiot.

19

Hickok stopped on the third step, smiling, slowly glancing to his left, then to his right. As he expected, Watchers were posted on the roofs of nearby structures, their M-16s at the ready. He counted three to his left, two to his right. That meant seven were still unaccounted for.

"I'm glad to see you have some sense," Captain Williams boomed from the cover of the park.

Hickok faced front, still grinning. He stared at Blade, puzzled. Were his eyes playing tricks on him, or was Blade moving?

"Where are the others?"

Stall. He had to stall, giving Geronimo and Bertha time to clamber down their makeshift rope, fall to the ground, and made their way around front.

"Where are the others?" Captain Williams repeated. *"I know there are more of you."*

"They're still inside," Hickok shouted.

"Tell them to come out, now!" Williams ordered.

"They don't trust you," Hickok yelled. "They're afraid you'll shoot them in the back."

"They have nothing to fear," Williams said,

sounding impatient.

"They don't know that," Hickok countered.

"We do not intend to kill you," Williams stressed. *"If they don't come out and drop their weapons, we will kill your friend."*

"Looks like we don't have much choice," Hickok admitted.

"Then you first. Drop your guns."

Hickok took two more steps, then paused. He'd given his Henry to Geronimo, leaving him the Colts and the Ruger, fully loaded. Eighteen shots didn't seem like much at a time like this.

"Drop your guns!" Williams barked. *"Now!"*

Hickok nodded and slowly lowered his hands, knowing the Watchers wouldn't expect him to match his revolvers against their M-16's, wouldn't anticipate anyone being that dumb, especially when he was so vulnerable, in the open, without any protection, so he could well imagine their surprise when he shifted to the right, drawing, the Pythons flashing from their holsters as he cocked the hammers, the Colts held waist high in the traditional gunfighter's stance, the two shots sounding as one.

The Watchers to his right, each on a different roof, disappeared from sight in a spray of blood and brains.

Hickok moved, the slugs from the M-16's already striking the concrete steps at his feet. He twisted and waved, dodged and spun, being as difficult a target as he could possibly be.

One of the shots tore a gash in the right side of his neck.

Another slug chipped his left heel.

Hickok reached the SEAL and whirled, firing each Python, and one of the Watchers to his left screamed, tumbling down the slanted roof and plummeting to the hard ground.

"Get the son of a bitch!"

Hickok dropped to the ground, rolling under the SEAL, relishing the temporary protection afforded by the transport's body, wishing he could stay where he was, but he couldn't, it wasn't part of his plan. He kept moving, coming out from under the vehicle on the side fronting the park, and he was up and running, heading for Blade, realizing it was do-or-die time.

A Watcher emerged from the vegetation, shouldering his M-16, taking precise aim.

Hickok let him have one in the head.

The Watchers were focusing all their firepower on the bobbing, spinning, twirling, and churning Warrior.

Another bullet hit home, biting into the gunman's left side.

Hickok slowed, ten yards from Blade, and snapped off shot at a Watcher directly ahead. The soldier went down, his hands over his face, shrieking and thrashing.

Blade abruptly came to life, his arms finally free. He stooped over, frantically tugging at the ropes binding his ankles.

Hickok heard a new gun enter the conflict, the blast of the Henry followed by Bertha's shotgun. He reached Blade's side, placing his body between Blade and the park. "Hurry it up, slowpoke!"

Three Watchers charged from the undergrowth, firing as they ran.

Hickok fired his right Colt twice, seeing one of the soldiers stumble and fall, and something ripped through his left shoulder. He staggered, dropping to his knees, flinging the empty right Colt aside and grabbing for the Ruger.

Somebody beat him to it.

Blade was suddenly at his side, leaning over him and drawing the Ruger, aiming at the remaining

Watchers.

Geronimo opened up with the Henry again.

The two Watchers were caught in a vicious cross fire, game to the very end, trying to shoot their foes even as slugs pierced their bodies, their faces contorted as they jerked from the impact. They landed on their stomachs, oozing blood, one of them gasping and wheezing from a shattered windpipe.

The firing suddenly ceased.

Geronimo and Bertha ran from the left side of the headquarters and joined their companions.

"Are you all right?" Bertha asked, placing her left hand on Hickok's shoulder. "You look pitiful."

"Thanks, Black Beauty," Hickok said wearily. "I needed that."

"Where are the rest?" Blade asked warily, scanning the park. "Or did we get them all?"

"By my calculations," Hickok replied, "there should be four of them left."

"Geronimo?" Blade said, running off. "The jeeps and the truck!"

Geronimo followed, alert for another attack from the park.

Hickok watched them go, his body aching. They were still in sight when the noise of engines cranking rent the dawn.

"They'll never make it," Bertha commented.

Hickok stood, his legs shaky.

"Hey, let me," Bertha said, using her right arm to support him around the waist. "How many times you been hit?"

"I lost count," Hickok replied.

"We'd best get you in to old Josh," Bertha stated, leading the gunman toward the steps. "He'll take care of you."

"Okay by me," Hickok agreed.

"You did real good, White Meat," Bertha

beamed. "I was proud of you."

"Piece of cake."

"I've never seen anyone handle a gun like you."

"Piece of cake."

"You sure say that a lot," Bertha noted. "Is it your favorite expression, or something?"

"I just like cake." Hickok grinned.

"You big dummy!" Bertha said affectionately.

They were half the distance to the SEAL when the heavy footsteps thudded behind them.

"What the . . . ?" Bertha began to turn, but something struck her across her chin, knocking her down.

Hickok crouched and whirled, his left Colt still gripped in his sweaty palm. Had one of the Watchers returned? If so, the Watcher had made a mistake because he still had some fight left in him and . . .

He froze, his eyes widening.

It was a massive male brute, caked with dried blood, its beady eyes ablaze, its gleaming teeth dripping with pink saliva. Wounds covered its torso.

Hickok managed to get off one shot before a brawny fist sent him to the ground.

The brute stood over its prey, clenching and unclenching its hands. Neither of them were the one he wanted.

Krill was after Blade.

Voices, raised in alarm, sounded to his rear.

Krill ran to the park, angling for the point where the vegetation bordered the street. A huge tree was closest to the roadway, and Krill slid behind the trunk as two men, Blade and another, raced by.

"It's Hickok and Bertha!" Geronimo exclaimed as they sighted their friends.

"But how . . ." Blade slowed, confused. They'd

caught a glimpse of the four Watchers making their getaway in a pair of jeeps, two soldiers to a vehicle. The remaining pair of jeeps, and the truck, were abandoned. Unless Hickok miscounted, the Watchers were all accounted for. So who had knocked Hickok and Bertha unconscious?

Krill roared as he sprang, reaching Geronimo in a single bound and slamming the Warrior to the pavement.

Blade raised the Ruger and fired once, the slug penetrating the brute's right chest area, the impact tugging Krill to the right, but the brute stayed on its feet and kept coming, snarling. Blade was caught in a bear hug and lifted off his feet. He jammed the barrel of the Ruger into Krill's right ear and pulled the trigger.

The Ruger was empty. He'd used five rounds on the two Watchers.

Krill growled as he attempted to crush the life from Blade. The brute smiled when Blade smashed the revolver barrel against his face. Krill wanted Blade to know there was no way to escape the inevitable. Krill desired sweet revenge for Arla.

Blade bashed the brute again and again, splitting the skin and busting the crooked nose, and still Krill maintained his pulverizing hold. He dropped the Ruger and crammed his palms under the brute's chin, striving to force the thick neck backward, to snap the spine. Krill's bullish neck barely budged.

Geronimo was suddenly there, one of his tomahawks in his right hand. He shouted his war whoop and plunged the tomahawk into the brute's neck.

Krill, shocked, enraged, flung Blade aside and pounced on Geronimo. The brute's neck injury was pouring blood, but Krill ignored the laceration and heaved the struggling Warrior into the air, completely over his head.

Geronimo landed with a pronounced thud.

Blade, lying on his right side, striving to collect his breath and gather his energy, glanced around. Hickok and Bertha were lying still, both rendered unconscious. Geronimo, momentarily stunned, was prone and motionless.

It was all up to him.

Blade labored to rise, his battered and bruised body sluggish in responding.

Krill was watching Blade, grinning and waiting.

"You must want me real bad," Blade muttered. He was astonished when the brute nodded.

"You can understand what I say?" Blade said, gawking.

Krill's smiled widened.

"But that's impossible . . ." Blade mumbled.

Krill pounced, reaching Blade in a single mighty bound. His huge hands gripped Blade's head and he began tugging, intending to literally tear Blade's head from his body.

Blade reacted automatically, reaching up and gouging his thumbs into the brute's eyes.

Krill released him and stumbled aside, rubbing his watery eyes, trying to clear his blurred vision.

Blade cast about for a weapon. He spied one of the tomahawks, on the ground near Geronimo, and ran to it, grabbing the handle, never stopping as he turned and closed on Krill, sweeping the tomahawk all the way back and, as he reached the brute, jumping as high as he could into the air while crashing the blade onto the top of the brute's head, completely burying it in Krill's cranium.

The brute sagged and collapsed on its knees, barely conscious.

Blade stepped back as Joshua ran up, holding the Browning. "Finish it off," Blade ordered. When Joshua went to object, Blade savagely poked him in the chest. *"Finish it now!"* he shouted.

Startled, bewildered at Blade's attitude, Joshua reluctantly placed the barrel against the brute's ear and pulled the trigger.

20

They were gathered in the headquarters building while Joshua ministered to their injuries.

"Josh the brute-slayer!" Hickok was teasing. "Has a ring to it!"

"Please." Joshua grimaced. "Don't remind me!"

"Wait until the Family hears about this," Hickok remarked. He was lying beside Bertha, near the bar. Blade was at the table, Geronimo standing guard.

"Please," Joshua addressed Hickok. "Don't inform the Family." He was bandaging Blade's wounds.

"Why not?" Hickok demanded.

"I simply don't want to be known as a . . ." he paused.

"As a killer," Hickok said, finishing the sentence for him.

"Exactly." Joshua nodded.

"You get used to it," Hickok informed Joshua.

Joshua stopped his ministrations and stared into Hickok's eyes. "Unlike you, I could never get used to it. Never."

"If that's what you want," Hickok said, shrugging, "it's fine by me. It'll be our little secret."

"So what's our next move?" Geronimo inquired.

"Do we have any choice?" Blade answered, flinching as Joshua applied a compress to his right shoulder.

"The beast took quite a bite out of you," Joshua noted.

"Yeah," Bertha cracked. "He and I have a lot in common!"

"As I was about to say," Blade commented, "I don't think we have any other choice. As I see it, we head for our Home instead of the Twin Cities. Anyone disagree?"

No one spoke.

"Fine." Blade nodded. "The Twin Cities will wait for another week or two, while we rest and recuperate." He stared at the floor, reflecting. It was funny. First, he had wanted to reach the Twin Cities as quickly as possible, and he had even persuaded Bertha to go along against her better judgment. Then, after Hickok and Bertha had been hurt, he had prevailed on them to return to the Home, using the pretext of their injuries, when in reality he wanted to see his darling Jenny again and ferret out the power-monger in the Family. It was as if he had looked for an excuse, any justification, for heading back. Now there was nothing else they could do. With three of them seriously wounded, the Twin Cities were definitely out of the question. It was funny, sometimes, how things worked themselves out.

"What about the truck and those jeeps?" Geronimo asked.

"What about them?" Blade inquired.

"Do we take one of them with us? The Family could really use another vehicle," Geronimo stated.

"Who'd drive it?" Blade inquired.

"I could do it," Hickok chimed in. "I've driven the SEAL before, you know."

"Except for one thing," Blade commented. "When Geronimo and I examined them earlier, I discovered both of the jeeps, and probably the truck too, are not like the SEAL."

"How so, pard?" Hickok questioned.

"The SEAL is what Plato called an automatic," Blade reminded him. "The Watcher's vehicles are not automatics. They're the old shift variety, using something called a clutch. I don't know how to drive one of those. Do you?"

"No," Hickok admitted. "But I could learn."

"We don't have the time," Blade said. "It's almost noon."

"The reinforcements aren't due until this evening," Hickok said. "Maybe I could learn by then."

"And what if they arrive sooner than expected?" Blade retorted. "What if they send an advance patrol? We're hardly in condition for another fight."

"Okay. So it's not such a hot idea," Hickok conceded. "No need to get all testy about it."

"Don't get me wrong," Blade corrected him. "I think it's a great idea, and if we had the time, and if we weren't in such lousy shape, I'd go for it. But . . ." He left the thought dangling.

"So what do we do?" Geronimo asked.

"We stick with the original plan," Blade answered. "We load up the generator and the supplies we confiscated, and whatever we can cram in from the truck, and take off for the Home."

"Don't forget the radio," Hickok added.

"That too. Anything I've forgotten?" Blade looked at each of them.

"There is one small thing . . ." Joshua said quietly.

"What is it?" Blade asked him.

"It's about the dead Watchers . . ."

"Oh no," Hickok groaned. "Here we go again."

"I don't suppose we could provide them with a proper burial?" Joshua inquired.

Blade shook his head. "I'm sorry, Joshua. We haven't got the time to spare."

"Just thought I'd ask," Joshua stated.

"Let's get cracking," Blade announced.

While Hickok and Geronimo retrieved the provisions hidden before the convoy arrived, Blade, with the assistance of Joshua and Bertha, dismantled the generator and the stereo. By three in the afternoon they had the supplies, the generator, various miscellaneous items, and a stack of M-16's piled into the transport, utilizing all the space available until there was scarcely room for *them*.

"I reckon it's about time, pard," Hickok said to Blade as they stood on the steps.

Blade nodded, his hands on his Bowies. He'd found his weapons stashed in the rear of the truck, and he had thanked the Spirit for the return of the long knives when he'd strapped them to his waist.

"The Family will be plumb tickled," Hickok commented.

"I'd like to know somethin'," Bertha said, coming through the door.

"What's that, Black Beauty?" Hickok asked her.

"How come you talk so funny sometimes?" Bertha inquired.

"Talk funny?" Hickok repeated.

Geronimo came through the door, laughing. "He does that because he's a fanatic about the Old West, as it was called in the books in our library," he explained. "Hickok likes to talk like he thinks they did way back then. You know, and I know, he sounds like a congenital idiot, but it's impossible to argue with a man who has rocks for brains."

"You're weird, White Meat." Bertha shook her head. "You're really weird."

"If you think he's weird now," Geronimo said, "then wait until you really get to know him."

"I don't understand why they always pick on me," Hickok said, lamenting his misfortune.

"Let's get out of here," Blade stated, smiling. He watched as they climbed into the SEAL, his eyes drifting over the park and the sky and the sun. The sun. He'd never be able to view the fiery orb in the same light again, not after what had happened. Each dawn, every new day, was so incredibly precious, so . . .

"Hey, pard, you coming?" Hickok called.

Blade walked to the transport and sat in the driver's seat.

"I can drive," Hickok offered, "if you don't feel up to it."

"I feel up to it," Blade assured him.

"Thank the Spirit!" Geronimo remarked. He was sitting in the front, cradling the Browning in his arms.

"I can't believe I'm really going to your Home," Bertha said longingly. "It's like a dream come true."

"You'll love it," Hickok verified. "I know."

"And you can bet I'll never leave it," Bertha announced for Blade's benefit. "Not ever!"

Blade started the motor and pulled out, glad he'd remembered to throw the red lever earlier. He wondered if Bertha had the right idea. The Home. Jenny. His Family. He'd been away from them twice, and each time he nearly lost his life. Only a fool would tempt fate three times running.

"It is a beautiful day," Joshua said softly.

"That it is," Blade heartily agreed, grinning happily. "Next stop, Home Sweet Home!"

TO BE CONTINUED IN:

THE ENDWORLD SERIES #3:

THE TWIN CITIES RUN